"It only fuels your reputation as a commitmentphobe who plays the field wildly—and those are not the kind of qualities that ordinary people want from the person who is representing them."

Emily met Alejandro's bright green gaze without flinching. "You need a wife, Alej. It would be an instant badge of commitment and respectability that would only help your career."

"But I don't want to get married," he observed caustically.

She shrugged. "An̶d̶ ̶t̶h̶a̶t̶'̶s̶ ̶y̶o̶u̶r̶ ̶d̶i̶l̶e̶m̶m̶a̶."

Yes.

His dilemma.

Or maybe not.

Maybe Emily was exactly what he needed. For now, at least. He'd thought she'd cared for him all those years ago but he'd been wrong, just as he'd been wrong about so many things.

Wouldn't marriage add a deliciously dark element to the revenge he was determined to exact on her? Wouldn't it ensure she would never really forget him, because what woman forgot the man who slid a golden ring onto her finger?

"I think you could be right, Emily," he said, slanting her a slow smile. "I need a temporary bride—and you are the obvious candidate."

Conveniently Wed!

Conveniently wedded, passionately bedded!

Whether there's a debt to be paid, a will to be obeyed or a business to be saved...she's got no choice but to say, "I do!"

But these billionaire bridegrooms have got another think coming if they imagine marriage will be that easy...

Soon their convenient brides become the objects of inconvenient desire!

Find out what happens after the vows in:

My Bought Virgin Wife by Caitlin Crews

The Sicilian's Bought Cinderella by Michelle Smart

Crown Prince's Bought Bride by Maya Blake

Chosen as the Sheihk's Royal Bride by Jennie Lucas

Penniless Virgin to Sicilian's Bride by Melanie Milburne

Untamed Billionaire's Innocent Bride by Caitlin Crews

Look for more Conveniently Wed! stories coming soon!

Sharon Kendrick

———

BOUGHT BRIDE FOR THE ARGENTINIAN

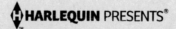

Recycling programs
for this product may
not exist in your area.

ISBN-13: 978-1-335-53845-1

Bought Bride for the Argentinian

First North American publication 2019

Copyright © 2019 by Sharon Kendrick

Printed in U.S.A.

Sharon Kendrick once won a national writing competition by describing her ideal date: being flown to an exotic island by a gorgeous and powerful man. Little did she realize that she'd just wandered into her dream job! Today she writes for Harlequin, and her books feature often stubborn but always *to-die-for* heroes and the women who bring them to their knees. She believes that the best books are those you never want to end. Just like life...

Books by Sharon Kendrick

Harlequin Presents

The Italian's Christmas Housekeeper

Conveniently Wed!

Bound to the Sicilian's Bed
The Greek's Bought Bride

One Night With Consequences

The Pregnant Kavakos Bride
The Italian's Christmas Secret
Crowned for the Sheikh's Baby

Secret Heirs of Billionaires

The Sheikh's Secret Baby

Wedlocked!

The Sheikh's Bought Wife

The Billionaire's Legacy

Di Sione's Virgin Mistress

Visit the Author Profile page
at Harlequin.com for more titles.

With special thanks to Melbourne-based Pat Conway for his invaluable insights into the high-octane world of Formula One—and a big shout-out to his dynamic wife, Chris.

Thanks also to equestrian genius Alison Clark, who inspired me with helpful details about polo and Argentina. Woof to Pop!

CHAPTER ONE

IT WAS WORSE than she'd thought. Much worse. Past and present merged into one heartbreaking reality as Emily buried her face into the rough texture of the horse's mane and wept. 'Oh, Joya,' she whispered. 'Whatever has become of you?'

The horse gave a weak whinny and Emily couldn't stem the tears even though she hadn't cried in a long time. Because tears got you nowhere. Crying didn't actually *change* anything, did it? It wasn't as if someone was going to suddenly turn up and wave a magic wand and make it all better. For a few moments she just stood there before forcing herseif to pull away, not wanting the animal to sense any more of the distress which had been swamping her ever since she'd arrived in this place.

Distractedly, she glanced around. A place which had been such a big part of her upbringing and was tied up with a swarm of memories. Bittersweet memories. Of a man with a hard body and warm, green eyes. A man who had brought her alive with his lips and his fingers and a whole lot else besides. Who had made her feel stuff she'd thought herself incapable of feeling. When she'd walked away from Alejandro Sabato it had felt as if someone were ripping her heart from her chest and then crushing it. In those few moments and all the months which had followed, she had truly known the definition of heartbreak. But she'd done it because there had been no other choice. Or at least it had seemed so at the time. Now she wondered if she had been a fool.

With an impatient hand she fisted away a tear, angry at herself for indulging in pointless reflection as she watched it tumble and soak into the rich Argentinian soil. Because she wasn't here to feel sad, or look back. And she certainly wasn't here to start thinking if only things had been different. Because there were no *if onlys* in life. The only certainty was that you took your choices and then had to live with the consequences, no matter how bleak they sometimes seemed.

She heard the sound of footsteps and turned to see Tomas walking slowly towards her, thinking how much the elderly retired groom had aged in the eight years since last she'd seen him. She had met him in the lawyer's office, and he and his wife had agreed to accompany her here today, insisting on bringing a bag of provisions to the now-empty house. She'd been pleased to have their company, yes—but, more importantly, pleased to have someone to share her shock at what had awaited them here.

Because the last time she'd stood on this spot, the estate had been thriving and the enormous ranch pristine and elegant. But not any more. Now it looked like a ragged ghost of a building, with none of its former glory remaining. Everywhere she looked she could see decay and neglect—from the overgrown veranda, where once socialites had laughingly sipped mint juleps, to the main house itself. Or what remained of it. There was no trace of the gleaming paintwork, near which had nestled fragrant white flowers amid glossy green leaves. A couple of upstairs windows were broken and one of the doors was falling off its hinges. Evidence of mice was everywhere in the empty and echoing rooms. And as for the stables... Well, they were something else.

Emily swallowed. There was nothing left of the stables other than the once-proud horse she had loved with all her heart, who now bore little resemblance to the powerful creature on which she had learnt to ride. Her body trembled with pain as she stroked his dusty coat.

'Oh, Tomas,' she said as the old groom reached her side. 'This is so *awful*.'

'*Sí, señorita,*' he agreed, his voice full of sadness.

'How on earth did it *happen*?'

Tomas gave a weary shrug. 'There was a little money left for his upkeep and I did what I could, but that money is now gone and the house is about to be sold to new owners who do not want him—or me. I would keep him if I could, but there is no room at my house for any animal—not even Joya.'

Emily dared to voice the fear which had been growing inside her ever since she'd walked in through the rusting gates of the property. 'Why on earth did my stepfather leave me the horse?' she demanded, but inside she suspected she knew why. It was to punish her. To lash out from beyond the grave and to cause her pain for daring to be the unwanted witness to his fiery marriage to her mother. The daughter he had never wanted, who had dared to fall in love with the son of the hired help.

Tomas was quiet for a moment and then

spoke with the authority of someone who had observed a great deal during the years he had worked at the huge estate.

'He bequeathed him to you because you loved him,' he said slowly.

Emily nodded. Yes. She had loved Joya. With all her heart she had adored that horse, who had been such an important part of her teenage years. She'd been taught to ride on that horse, by the man with the green eyes and the hard body. She'd sought refuge from her mother's hysteria by galloping out over the lush green of the Argentinian landscape for hours on end. And it was hard to see the welfare of a creature you loved threatened like this.

Yet she'd hardly followed his progress avidly in the years since the divorce and her mother's subsequent death, had she? She had cut her ties with Argentina ruthlessly for all kinds of reasons, but now fate had brought her back to this vast land and she was shocked by what she had found. 'I can't bear the thought that Joya might have to be...*put down*, Tomas,' she whispered. 'I've racked my brain and tried to come up with some kind of solution but I can't think of anything.'

She had expected gloomy agreement but,

surprisingly, the grooves on Tomas's weath-
ered skin began to deepen as, unexpectedly,
he smiled. 'But there is a solution, *señorita*,'
he said. 'And it has arrived sooner than even
I imagined.'

He was looking at the sky as he spoke. The
clear, blue Argentinian sky. It took a moment
for Emily to realise that its unspoiled surface
had been marred by the tiniest black spot in
the distance, which was growing bigger all
the time, and that a peace-shattering buzzing
sound was gradually getting louder.

Shielding her gaze against the brightness of
the sun with the flat of her hand, she frowned.
'What's that?' she questioned, even though it
was perfectly obvious what it was. A flashy-
looking helicopter, and it was heading this
way. A sudden inner misgiving made her skin
grow cold, despite the heat of the day.

'My prayers have been answered,' said
Tomas emotionally. 'For he flies to us like a
bird of prey! *El cóndor!*'

It was then that goosebumps began to ripple
over Emily's body as if an icy wind had suddenly started whipping through the warm day,
and she wrapped her bare arms tightly over her
chest as if to protect herself. Her heart started
to pound as the helicopter grew closer and she

watched it hover overhead before beginning its swaying descent. She wanted to run as far as her feet would take her. To seek refuge from the dark figure she could see seated at the controls, displaying the kind of powerful mastery which had always been so much a part of his appeal. But not all of it, no, she reminded herself painfully. He had been tender, too—and it had been that tenderness which had been her undoing. He had demonstrated an affection which had been like a revelation to her, for she had never experienced anything like it before. And hadn't it been that more than anything else which had made her fall head over heels in love with him? Hadn't it been that which had made the pain of leaving him so bitterly hard to bear?

During the intervening years since their last tumultuous meeting, Alejandro Sabato had become an icon and international heartthrob. He had dramatically ended his career as a world-class polo player—though nobody knew why—but hadn't taken any of the usual paths after leaving the sport behind. No riding schools or polo club for him. Instead he had become a hugely successful businessman who operated on a global scale, though he'd never been able to shake off the stormy reputation which had grown up after a bitter book written by his ex-mistress.

But Emily didn't associate him with riches beyond most people's wildest dreams. She remembered him as the man who used to slowly trace the line of her lips with his fingertip before bending his head to kiss her. The man who had taught her the true meaning of love.

And she had thrown it all back in his face.

The wind created by the clattering craft was flattening the grasses and playing havoc with her hair, even though she'd tied it back into a plait when she'd stumbled out of bed that morning, still jet-lagged after her long flight. Her jeans were clean but that was pretty much all you could say about them, and her T-shirt was plain and unremarkable. Briefly, she wondered why she was worrying about her appearance at a time like this. But deep down she knew why.

Because he had been her lover.

Her only lover.

The man to whom she'd given her innocence, and in doing so had sealed her empty fate for ever.

She smoothed a flapping strand of hair away from her cheek, wishing she could quell the painful thundering of her heart. She hadn't realised he could pilot a helicopter, but that shouldn't have come as any surprise. Hadn't he gone from being a dirt-poor boy who possessed an extraordinary gift with horses to becoming one of the world's richest men? Financial success stuck to his skin like stardust—but not personal success, she reminded herself. The newspapers always described him as a playboy and commitment-phobe—as a man who had left countless broken hearts in his arrogant wake.

The rotor blades slowed to a halt and as the door of the craft opened, Alejandro Sabato leapt to the ground. He landed with a light thud, giving a brief masterclass in agility and strength and reminding her of his nickname earned during his polo-playing days—*el cóndor*—the one which Tomas the groom had just breathed in wonder. Emily swallowed. They used to call him that because he was dark and menacing and because he used to swoop down like a graceful predator, always getting the ball he was chasing. He'd been on the winning side of three World Polo Championships—and it had always been Alejandro who was pictured holding the trophy aloft, his dark head thrown back, his face grinning with victory and vitality.

Yet he had started out from the most humble of places—the illegitimate son of her stepfather's housekeeper who, from the age of three, had grown up on his ranch and learned to ride almost as soon as he could walk. His talent had been spotted early and he'd moved to a polo stable on the other side of the country, where he had been intensively schooled in the sport. Six years older than Emily, he returned to the ranch only infrequently and she'd met him first at the age of twelve, soon after her mother had married Paul Vickery.

Had he recognised how lonely and out of place the English city girl had felt in that sweeping great country, in the home of a man who didn't really want a stepdaughter? Was that why he'd been so kind to her? He'd taught her to ride—and to recognise the stars. He'd given her *yerba maté* to drink and taught her how to light a fire and then how to put it out again safely. A friendship had grown between them, although inevitably she had grown to idolise him. And then, when she was seventeen, something had shifted and changed. Desire had entered into their easy camaraderie and nothing was ever the same again.

But that was a long time ago. They'd both lived a lot of life and were adults now. Yet

Emily found herself standing watching as Alejandro raked his windswept waves back from his forehead and the clench of her heart reminded her just how much he had meant to her. Suddenly a wave of nerves was rushing through her and she felt as if she were back in the shoes of that gauche young girl who had so adored him.

He must have seen her but he completely ignored her, going instead to Tomas and gripping him in a bear hug, before slipping into a stream of velvety Spanish, which caused the aging groom to beam with delight. Emily's command of the language was rusty these days but she understood enough to realise that Alej was making a request for refreshment and Tomas nodded and began to walk slowly towards the house, presumably to relay the message to his wife, Rosa.

And once the groom had disappeared, the two of them were alone and just at that moment the sun disappeared behind a cloud, so that all the light and warmth seemed to leave the day. Slowly, the Argentinian turned around to survey her with a look which was cold. So cold. She was shocked at how the vibrancy seemed to have left the gaze she remembered so well. How his once-warm green eyes were now like leaves which had been coated in ice and the curl of his lips bordered on contemptuous. Yet that didn't stop her breasts from tightening beneath her cotton shirt, or a long-forgotten hint of awareness from rippling sweetly over her thighs.

'Alej!' she said, the word much shakier than she would have liked—but there was no answering smile in response.

'Only my close friends and intimates call me that these days,' he corrected coolly, the curve of his mouth flattening into a cruel, hard line. 'Let's stick to Alejandro, shall we?'

It hurt, as it was probably intended to do, but Emily nodded as if it didn't. As if all those years of friendship and companionship and then love had never happened. As if the man who'd used to suck on her breasts as if they were freshly peeled grapes had just made the most reasonable of requests. She'd learnt many things over the years but one of the most important was to keep pain hidden away, where nobody could see it.

'Of course,' she responded, before adding a somewhat flippant amendment of her own. 'It's probably the shock of seeing you again, *Alejandro.*'

'Would you really describe it as a shock,

Emily?' he questioned, his richly accented voice thoughtful. 'Or a deep and abiding pleasure? From the darkening of your eyes and the tension in your body I recognise so well, I would guess it's the latter.'

Emily worked in PR, so she knew everything there was to know about putting a positive spin on things, but never had an upbeat mindset seemed so distant as it did right then. He was talking to her with sensuality dripping from every word, yet he was staring at her with a flicker of contempt in his green eyes, as if she meant nothing. And yet that didn't seem to have any effect on her reaction to *him*. All the feelings she'd thought were dead and buried started bubbling up inside her and she couldn't seem to stem them, no matter how hard she tried. She wanted to feast her eyes on the liquorice-black waves of his just-too-long hair and the burnished bronze of his glowing skin. Just as she wanted to ogle his body in the way that someone who'd been wandering around in the desert for days might stare greedily at a cool flask of water. And most of all she wanted to hurl herself into his arms and kiss him.

Concentrating very hard, she fixed him with an expression of polite curiosity, trying to behave as if he was someone she'd just met. But her outward calm didn't mirror what was happening inside, because suddenly it felt as if her hormones had remembered what they'd been designed for. As if his presence had the power to make her body prickle with desire and heat and expectation. Her nipples were thrusting uncomfortably against her bra and she felt a long-forgotten twist of lust low in her groin as she looked at him.

In the past he'd always worn jodhpurs or faded jeans, which hugged his hips and thighs in a way which had seemed indecently provocative. But not today. Today, clad in an immaculate lightweight suit, he was looking like the billionaire he'd become—not the rookie polo player she'd fallen in love with, who'd barely had two pesos to rub together. And love was the last thing she needed to think about if she was going to get through this, she reminded herself fiercely. She needed to find out what had prompted his unexpected appearance and then for him to leave as quickly as possible. She certainly didn't need to respond to his provocative observations about her body. Even if they happened to be true.

'Why are you here, Alejandro?' she questioned, instantly becoming aware of the slight edge to her voice and trying her best to iron it out. 'Why have you turned up out of the blue?' Briefly, she cast her gaze towards the sky. 'Quite literally in this case?'

'Don't play games, Emily,' he said softly. 'It's a waste of both our time. I came because you need me.'

Emily blinked very fast. 'I *need* you?'

'Are you going to repeat everything I say?' His voice was silky. 'Haven't you grown out of that kind of docile behaviour by now?'

Don't react to that either, she told herself. You don't need to get into a fight with him. You're no longer that giddy teenager who used to follow him around like a tame dog and lap up everything he said to you. And you're not the young woman who cried every night for months after she'd walked away. You left that person behind a long time ago. You became somebody else. Somebody grown-up and to-gether.

So Emily tilted her chin in the way she'd learned from watching other women. The way which sent out a message to the world that you were super-confident, even if inside you won-dered why you couldn't ever seem to lose that little stone of sadness which was buried deep inside you.

'I'm not here to trade insults, Alejandro,' she

said calmly. 'I asked you a perfectly reasonable question about why you were here.'

For a moment his green eyes narrowed. 'Tomas emailed me. I assumed with your blessing.'

She screwed up her brow in a frown. 'What did the email say?'

He shrugged and she wished he hadn't because it made her uncomfortably aware of the iron-hard muscle which lay beneath the fine silk of his shirt. Just as it made her aware of the rocky power of the arms which used to hold her so tightly, so that all the troubles of the world seemed to ebb away.

'That your stepfather had died—which I already knew, obviously, since news travels fast—and that he had bequeathed you your old horse. And since you didn't have the means to look after him, you were desperate for someone to step in and help you out.' He stared at her. 'Is that true?'

Desperate? Was she? Emily met the question in his piercing green gaze. She was certainly still reeling from the recent events which had recently turned her life upside down. Her loathsome stepfather had finally paid the price for his long-standing love affair with the bottle and had died a lonely death, which she couldn't really be sad about. She hadn't seen him since the bitter events following his acrimonious divorce from her mother and had been shocked to find herself listed as a beneficiary of his will. She still wondered what had possessed her to beg her business partner for some unplanned leave and then to turn up in a dusty lawyer's office in Buenos Aires to discover what he had left her. Was it simply curiosity or just a sudden desire to lay to rest the ghosts of her past?

Either way, she had been disappointed. It seemed there had been no deathbed conversion which had made Paul Vickery want to make amends for the harsh treatment he'd meted out to her and her mother. It had been just another twist of the knife really.

'Some of it is true,' she said huskily. 'My stepfather *did* leave me Joya. But no way did I ask Tomas to get in touch with you. You're the last person I'd ever choose to contact.'

Alejandro's mouth flattened as her soft English voice washed over him. Of course he was. He was disposable, wasn't he? A poor boy with a hard body who could be dispensed with once he'd done his job as stud. He had been deemed suitable enough to introduce her to the art of pleasure and then afterwards tossed aside like a piece of trash. And Emily Green had played him for a fool, hadn't she? Stared at him with those big sapphire eyes. Tossed her fair hair like a feisty pony, so that it rippled down her back like a field of golden wheat. He'd been transfixed by her Englishness. By her pale beauty and the pert vigour of her young body. Long legs and slender arms and a pale bottom, which curved like the moon.

She'd driven him mad with frustration and desire those hot summer nights when he'd lain alone on his narrow bunk next to the stables, sweat pouring from his brow and his groin close to bursting as he imagined losing himself in all her sweet, secret places. And then, when his dream had finally come true and he had bedded her at last—she had turned around and crushed his honour and his hopes beneath one of her costly leather shoes, before walking away from him without a backward glance.

At the time he had been astonished by her behaviour—but not for long. Because soon after that he was to discover that all women were liars and cheats. But it had been Emily who had hurt him the most, who had wielded the sharpest blade, which felt like it was digging deep into his heart. And didn't they say that the first cut was the deepest?

'So what are you planning to do?' he said, slanting a compassionate look towards the horse who was still trying to summon up the strength to nuzzle Emily's hand. 'Put a bullet to his head?'

She recoiled, staring at him as if he had just ascended from the depths of hell.

'Are you advocating I kill my horse?' she accused shakily. 'You, who always loved animals?'

'Yes, I loved them and still do,' he grated. 'More than I ever loved any human, that's for sure—and way too much to want to condemn them to a life of neglect. Is that what you want for Joya, Emily? For his eyes to grow so dull that he can barely see and he doesn't even have the strength to put food in his mouth?'

'Of course that's not what I want,' she declared, the quick shake of her head drawing his eyes reluctantly to the thick shimmer of her blonde hair. 'But I don't have...'

'Don't have what?' he prompted silkily.

Emily stared at him, not wanting to divulge the truth—not to him of all people. But what good was pride in a situation like this? Shouldn't she be thinking about Joya, rather than how humble her life must appear to this new and very different Alejandro, who breathed wealth and power from every pore of his spectacular body?

'I don't have the means to look after him,' she admitted. 'I live in a small apartment in the middle of London and I couldn't possibly move him there—'

'I doubt he would survive the journey anyway.'

She nodded, wishing he hadn't made the curt intervention because she didn't need reminding of how frail Joya was. 'I also have a very modest lifestyle,' she continued, a rush of blood heating her cheeks as he continued to look at her with a trace of scorn. 'Which certainly wouldn't allow me to fund Joya's care here in Argentina.'

He appeared to be mulling over her words when Rosa appeared on the veranda carrying a couple of the wooden drinking cups known as gourds, and Emily felt a quick pang of nostalgia as she recognised the traditional Argentinian drink of *yerba maté*. Because it had been Alejandro who'd first introduced her to it—showing her how to suck it up out of the straw-like strainer, which prevented the leaves from clogging up your mouth. Who had told her laughingly that if she wasn't careful, the caffeine would keep her awake all night—but that was okay by him. She remembered how cosmopolitan he'd made her feel and how the whisper of his fingertips over her skin had made her stomach turn to jelly.

'Why don't we go over to the veranda and have this discussion in the shade, while Tomas takes Joya back to the stables?' Alejandro suggested smoothly.

To Emily's surprise she found herself agreeing, even though instinct was telling her it might not be such a great idea. Maybe it was the shock of seeing him again which made her follow him up the old wooden steps. Or maybe it was just that old habits died hard, because she'd always been a sucker for his suggestions. Either way, she was glad to take a seat on the veranda, taking a thirsty pull of the bitter drink Rosa had left for them.

Once her thirst had been quenched, she became aware of the Argentinian's cool gaze fixed on her and she fidgeted a little. He had undone a third button on his white shirt and was stretching his long legs in front of him, drawing her attention to the taut fabric of his trousers, which stretched across the muscular definition of his hard thighs. She could feel beads of sweat breaking out on her forehead as she found herself remembering those thighs hair-roughened and naked as they thrust against the smoothness of her own skin. Yet their physical relationship had been cut abruptly short, she reminded herself, wondering how something so brief could have had such an enduring impact. And then she remembered something else.

'Tomas told me that your mother had died last year,' she said quietly. 'I'm very sorry for your loss.'

It was then that his face changed. She watched it darken with anger and she shrank back a little against the battered wicker chair.

'You are hypocritical enough to express your condolences?' he demanded. 'When it was your spite which meant my mother lost her job?'

CHAPTER TWO

THE LOUD SWELL of the cicadas was the only sound which could be heard above the loud beat of her pounding heart as Emily stared at Alejandro across the faded veranda. 'I don't know what you're talking about,' she breathed. 'How could I have possibly been responsible for your mother losing her job?'

He sliced his hand through the air with a gesture of disdainful impatience. 'Don't give me that false wide-eyed look of innocence, Emily.'

'It's not false. It's genuine. I don't know what you're talking about.'

His brow darkened, his green gaze narrowing. 'After we were discovered together and you flew back to England as if the hounds of hell were at your heels, my mother was called into your father's study and told to leave the property immediately, never to return.' His face contorted with contempt. 'Twenty-one years of devotion thrown back in her face.'

Emily's lips fell open and she shook her head in vehement denial. 'I swear I didn't know that. I thought she'd left of her own accord.'

'Oh, come on. Women of such subservience don't just *leave of their own accord*,' he mimicked cruelly. 'Did you know your stepfather refused to provide any references for her, so she couldn't get any more work? And although I was able to provide some means of support, she complained that her life felt empty without work.'

Alejandro felt his mouth harden with anger and frustration. He had wanted to help his mother in more practical ways than simply buying her a small house. Having given birth to him at just seventeen, she'd been young enough to retrain in something different. Young enough to start again. But she hadn't wanted a new life. She had just smoked cigarette after cigarette while continuing to spin him the same old lies, which for a time while he'd been growing up had made him feel special and different. And wasn't it crazy that he'd hung onto the myth he'd been spun for so long—so that when he had finally learned the truth, it had nearly broken him?

He stared at Emily. Maybe it was true what she said and she hadn't been directly responsible for his mother's sacking, but that didn't change the anger he felt towards her, did it? Because he had loved her in a way he had never loved anyone else and he'd thought she loved him, too. But she hadn't. She had been the only woman who had ever rejected him and she had done it in a cruel and dismissive manner which had emphasised his subservient status. He would never forget the way she had looked through him, as if he had been invisible. *As if he were nothing.* Was it that which had planted the bitter seed of anger, deep in the empty place he called his heart?

He watched as, with an unsteady hand, she put down her half-empty gourd and fixed him with those incredible sapphire eyes of hers.

'You still haven't explained what brought you here today, Alej.'

He leaned his head back against the chair and surveyed her from between slitted eyes. 'Because I think I can help you. Or rather, I think we can help each other.'

She shook her head. 'After the things you've just accused me of, I'm amazed you're offering, but I'll decline if it's all the same to you.'

She gritted him a polite smile. 'I don't need your help.'

'Oh, I think you do,' he contradicted softly. 'That is, if you want to save Joya. If you'd like him to live out his days happily in a flower-filled meadow, with a loving groom to tend to his every need rather than ending up on the scrapheap, which is where he's heading right now.'

'Are you trying to use an old, sick horse in order to blackmail me?'

'Not at all. I'm simply stating facts,' he said. 'And suggesting we do a trade-off.'

Still reeling from the fact that he held her responsible for his mother's sacking, Emily wondered what on earth he was talking about. Because what could someone like her do for someone like him, when he was an iconic billionaire and she was…? She stared down at her jeans and canvas sneakers. At the unmanicured hands which were resting on the sides of the chair. She was just an ordinary woman trying to find some balance after a tumultuous upbringing, which had bounced her round like a rubber ball. A woman who had been chasing independence since she'd graduated from college. Normality was what she craved more than anything and contact with Alejandro Sabato certainly wouldn't go anywhere towards helping her achieve that aim. Because he made her want something it was dangerous to want and that something was him. He made her think of slow touching and long kissing—both of which she'd like to do right now, even though he was looking at her with an expression of barely veiled contempt. And hadn't that been the root cause of her mother's tragic story—that she had been hooked on a man who had secretly despised her? Did she really want the same thing for herself?

Her instinct was to finish her drink, to smile politely and tell him she would manage somehow. She would find a way to save Joya, though she wasn't quite sure how she was going to go about it in a country which now felt distinctly foreign to her, despite having spent so much time here.

But Argentina was Alej's homeland, wasn't it? If anyone knew how best to deal with re-homing an ancient horse and rescuing him from certain death, it was him. And because he looked so powerful and dependable as he sat opposite her on the shaded veranda, she found the words leaving her mouth before she'd had time to consider the wisdom of saying them. 'What kind of trade-off?' she questioned cautiously.

Reflectively, he stirred his drink with the *bombilla* before lifting his gaze to hers, rugged features darkened by the shade cast by the overgrown shrubs which tumbled down the side of the veranda. 'How much do you know about me, Emily?'

It was an unexpected question and Emily wished he hadn't asked it. Because she knew him intimately, as only a lover could. His hard body. That low, exultant moan he'd given as he had bucked to fulfilment—over and over during that night. The only night. Flustered, she shrugged, trying to dredge up some of the facts she'd buried deep in her mind, where she rarely allowed herself to venture. 'I know you came from a poor family and that your mother—'

'No, not back then,' he interrupted, and suddenly there was a bitterness about him which she'd never seen before. Or maybe she just hadn't hung around long enough to see it.

'Spare me the rags-to-riches story which has been told a million times,' he ordered roughly. 'I'm talking about modern day. Real time. Now.'

Emily screwed up her eyes. If she admitted to knowing stuff about his current lifestyle, mightn't that seem as if she was somehow *trolling* him, like some sad ex-lover who couldn't bear to let go? But Alejandro Sabato wasn't just anyone, she reminded herself. Everything he touched made headlines—both work *and* play. Who *hadn't* heard of him?

'I know you suddenly retired from polo,' she said. 'And that your decision took everyone by surprise.'

He nodded but provided no explanation. His verdant gaze just continued to cut through her, like a knife slicing through a ripe melon. 'What else?'

She hesitated. After all the drama and fallout she'd experienced while growing up, she tried not to place too much importance on wealth—but in this case that would be like trying to ignore a whole herd of elephants who were trying to trample their way into a small cupboard. Especially with that top-of-the-range black helicopter, which was shining like a giant beetle in the field not far from where they were sitting, and the fact that Alejandro had recently come in at number thirty-four on a list of the world's richest men.

'That you invested in an energy drink which is pretty much drunk everywhere and used some of the money you made to help a friend set up a social media app. And then you bought into a motor-racing team, which has reaped its own rewards,' she offered. 'So you've exchanged one kind of high-intensity sport for another.'

'Very neatly summarised,' he said, raising his dark eyebrows. 'Perhaps I should be flattered that you've taken such an interest in my progress, Emily.'

'Please don't be,' she said sharply. 'I work in PR and it's my job to read the papers. And since you take up a lot of column space in the international press, it's hardly surprising that I should have picked up some facts about you over the years.'

From the thick lashes which framed the startling green eyes, he continued to survey her. 'Then you will know about Colette?'

There was the briefest of pauses before Emily nodded, surprised by how much it hurt to hear him say another woman's name. 'Doesn't everyone? Supermodels of her stature are few and far between. I gather you broke up,' she added blandly. 'And she wrote an unauthorised biography about you.'

'Did you read it?'

Emily shook her head. Was he mad? Of course she hadn't read it! She'd seen the title and hadn't even been able to face giving it a quick skim-through. Because what woman would want to absorb details of her ex-lover's wild sex life with one of the world's hottest supermodels? 'No,' she said, and then—because he seemed to be waiting for more—she forced herself to continue. 'But I gather it wasn't favourable towards you.'

Alej almost smiled. He'd forgotten the English penchant for understatement, just as he'd forgotten how Emily's cool beauty had the ability to ignite something deep inside him. It always had. He hadn't seen her in eight years, yet the lust which was pulsing through his body was as powerful as it had been when he'd met her way back when. Back then, she had been forbidden fruit for all kinds of reasons. Too young, for a start—even before you factored in that she was the stepdaughter of his mother's employer and that nobody in their right mind would dare mess around with the boss's family.

But desire was a powerful driver. It had eaten him up from the inside out. Plagued and tormented him like a fever, so that he'd had to work extra hard to concentrate on the polo which had always consumed him and had promised a route out of the poverty into

which he'd been born. And wasn't the truth
that Emily hadn't been like the other girls who
hung around the polo field with their breasts
practically falling out of their shirts? An out-
and-out tomboy, she'd somehow made him *feel*
stuff. Stuff he wasn't used to feeling, which
had made him want to buy her flowers and
brush her hair in the moonlight and tell her
that her skin was paler than the stars. He'd
thought it had been the same for her—that she
had reciprocated his see-sawing emotions during those long months of stolen kisses and fur-
tive embraces before he had finally made love
to her.

His groin hardened. Because of her innocence and relative youth he had employed an
uncharacteristic restraint around Emily Green.
It had almost killed him to hold off until her
eighteenth birthday, though in the end they had
missed it by a day because they just couldn't
wait any longer. Never had a sexual build-up
been so exquisitely slow or sweetly torturous,
so that when he had finally slipped inside her,
he'd come almost as quickly as she had done.
He'd been having safe sex with willing part-
ners since the age of sixteen—but nothing
could have prepared Alej for his first time with
Emily, when he plunged deep into her tight and

molten heat. The only time, he reminded himself bitterly, before forcing his attention back to
the present and the sapphire-blue eyes which
were regarding him with a curiosity which was
somehow adding to his frustration and long-
suppressed anger.

'It was, as you say—an unfavourable piece,'
he conceded, his temperate tone at odds with
his turbulent thoughts. 'But, unfortunately,
mud sticks and she told a lot of lies about me.'

She tilted her head to one side, so that her
thick blonde plait fell forward and lay enticingly against the firm thrust of her breasts.
'What kind of lies?'

'What man would wish to list their supposed
transgressions to another woman? Why don't
you just read the book for yourself?' There was
a pause. 'And in the meantime, I could make
sure that Joya is taken care of.'

Her attention was momentarily distracted as
she watched a lizard slithering its way across
the decking before looking up at him.

'That's a very generous offer,' she said un-
certainly.

'Which obviously isn't motivated simply by
my love of horses.'

'No?'

He shook his head and gave a glimmer of a

smile. 'Of course not. I expect to extract a reward for my benevolence.'

Behind the smile an undeniable threat was
underpinning his words and as Emily stared
into his eyes she felt a sudden chill whisper
its way over her skin. If she hadn't been so
worried and in such a helpless position about
helping Joya, she wouldn't have needed to
ask the question, but the reality was that she
did. 'What kind of "reward" did you have in
mind?'

The slow smile he flicked her was tinged
with sensual promise, but the words which followed were the last thing Emily was expecting to hear.

'You work in public relations, don't you?'

She blinked. 'How did you know that?'

'It wasn't difficult. I did a little research,
before you arrived. Your reputation is modest, but it's growing. I read nothing but good
things about you.' There was a brief pause. 'So
how about you come and work for me, as my
PR representative?'

'You don't have one at the moment?'

'Never saw the need.' He shrugged. 'But if
you can polish my tarnished image for me,
then we'll call it quits.'

'But why?' Her brow creased into a frown. 'I

mean, why do you suddenly care what people think about you when you never did before?'

He didn't answer for a moment and when he did his voice was reflective. 'Because I'm thinking of throwing my hat into the political ring and my current reputation will do me no favours. If you can make this bad-boy billionaire into a respectable member of polite society, I will reward you very handsomely.'

Emily stared at him. Was he actually *offering her a job*? Asking her to create a squeaky-clean image for him, which would involve her delving into aspects of his life which made her feel ill just thinking about them? She couldn't do it. In fact, she wouldn't do it. You could only ever take a job like this if you were properly impartial and impartiality was the last thing she felt towards the Argentinian billionaire.

She shook her head. 'I don't think you realise how my kind of business operates, Alejandro,' she said. 'I can't suddenly start working exclusively for you—even if I wanted to, which I don't. I have commitments.'

His hand sliced through the air with that same impatient gesture. 'I'm not interested in the detail. I've told you what I want, so make it happen. Leave your job if necessary.'

'Leave my job?' Her lips fell open. 'I'm in

partnership with a friend from uni. That's just not possible.'

'Anything is possible, Emily,' he bit out. 'We both know that. We live in a world where a poor illegitimate boy can rise up the greasy pole to have more money than he knows what to do with.'

She shook her head. 'Find someone else, Alejandro. There are plenty of public relations officers who are of an equally high standard who would bite your hand off to get this kind of job.'

'But they aren't you,' he said silkily. 'Are you haggling with me because you want to obtain the highest price for your services—is that what this is all about? In which case, let me tell you something which might influence your opinion.'

He mentioned a sum of money which took her breath away. Emily dug her fingers into the arms of the wicker chair and levered herself up, needing to get away from his distracting gaze as she tried to process the offer he'd just made her. That was a *lot* of money. Walking over to the edge of the veranda, she stared out at the lush Argentinian landscape and the cotton-wool clouds which were billowing up on the horizon.

She knew she ought to refuse because only a fool would accept—given their history. She'd hurt him for no reason other than that she'd been scared. But she had reasons for being tempted by the money—and not just because her embryo PR business could do with a financial cushion. And there was Great-Aunt Jane to think about—her only living relative who Emily kept a tender eye on as often as she could. Because her pension was tiny, wasn't it? She had become one of those old people who were scared of the future because they weren't quite sure if they would have enough money to fund whatever lay ahead. Wouldn't it be great if she could take away some of her worries by presenting her with a generous cheque?

But deep down Emily knew that her eagerness to accept Alejandro's offer was about more than helping care for a dear relative. The truth was that for too long she'd felt as if she was existing on some kind of plateau. As if life was passing her by. These days she rarely dated but when she did, she felt *empty*. As if she'd been carved from stone. And the reason for that was standing right in front of her. Tall, dark and indomitable. The man who made all other men seem as insubstantial as shadows.

The man who made the idea of loving someone else seem impossible.

Sometimes she suspected that she'd ide-
alised Alejandro Sabato and allowed time to
distort her memory of him, although the reality of seeing him in the flesh was as powerful
as it had ever been. But if she'd been guilty
of putting him on a pedestal, then surely here
was the perfect opportunity to dismantle it. To
see for herself the man he really was, rather
than the superhero of her young and lovestruck
imagination. She could feel the thunder of her
heart as she tried to imagine it. Wouldn't daily
contact with the arrogant billionaire reinforce
all the reasons why it was the best decision to
walk away, as well as saving Joya and helping
her great-aunt in the process?

She turned back to find him looking at her
and the most stupid thing was that all she really wanted was for him to hold her. To cradle
her in his strong arms and make her feel truly
desired again. Determinedly, she pushed those
thoughts away.

'Since I can't see any alternative,' she said
slowly, 'I'll take the job.'

Alejandro felt a beat of anger because he'd
seen the way her eyes had lit up like a Christmas tree when he'd mentioned the money. It

seemed she was just like her mother, he observed bitterly—available to the highest bidder. Yet she wore no outward signs of the wealth she clearly craved. Her clothes were decidedly unsexy and her face bare of make-up. He wondered if she had been disappointed with the laughable legacy left to her by her stepfather and was surprised how much pleasure it gave him to hope so.

'I thought that might sway it,' he remarked, raking his fingers back through the thick tumble of his hair. 'There are very few women who aren't persuaded by the prospect of instant wealth.'

And then he remembered why he was here—not to stand in judgement or to remind himself that she was shallow and avaricious. The real reason was as old as time itself. She had hurt him. Badly. And now it was time to hurt her right back.

He flicked her a smile. 'I'm flying out to Australia for the Melbourne Grand Prix next week and I want you there,' he said silkily.

She nodded as she looked up, her expression composed, but he sensed an inner tension about her which echoed his own. He could see those blue eyes widening. Darkening. He could see the almost surreptitious way that the tip of her tongue slid out to moisten the lush cushion of her lower lip. Soon, he thought, with a beat of anticipation. Soon he would make her realise what she was missing and how stupid she had been to turn her back on him in such a cold and callous manner.

And then he could walk away.

His mouth hardened.

For ever.

CHAPTER THREE

'EMILY, ARE YOU OKAY? I mean, seriously?' Marybeth's voice was full of concern. 'I've never seen you like this before, not in all the years I've known you.'

Slowly Emily turned around to survey her business partner, who'd been her best friend since they'd met during their final year of college. Still reeling from her mother's sudden death, Emily had been floundering when Marybeth Miller had swooped in and taken her under her wing. She'd insisted on bringing Emily back for weekends at her family's rambling farmhouse in north Devon, where Emily had come into contact with the kind of noisy, good-hearted atmosphere she'd never known before. It had been her first experience of teasing siblings and walking for miles in the fresh country air before sitting down to eat enormous hunks of home-made cake, and it had helped her come to terms with her bereavement, though that hadn't been easy.

Her pain had been compounded by other feelings: by guilt and regret—but especially guilt. She kept wondering if she could have done something to stop her mother's inevitable decline. If she could maybe have stopped her taking tranquillisers or shown her that there was a life worth living, even as a divorcee. But alongside the guilt had come a rush of something else and Emily hadn't been able to shake off her relief that she was now liberated from all the emotional trauma of her mother's life. She wondered if it had been that liberation which had prompted her to mail Alejandro a letter, apologising for everything that had happened and offering a cautious olive branch, suggesting that if he was playing in England any time soon, then perhaps they could meet up for a drink. But he hadn't even bothered to reply. And maybe part of her couldn't blame him. Did she really imagine that the proud Argentinian would share a cocktail with her after she'd dumped him so brutally?

'I mean, look at you now—you're *miles* away!' Marybeth was staring at Emily in bemusement. 'And you've got this look on your face, like...'

'Like what?' Emily prompted curiously.

'You're all wired,' said her friend. 'As if someone's turned on a light inside you and you've suddenly come alive. Yet you look scared, too. As if something's waiting just around the corner for you and you don't like what it is.' She paused. 'You know, you don't have to accept this job from this guy Alejandro Sabato.'

Emily gave a hollow laugh. 'What, and turn down the best money and exposure we've ever been offered just because I once stupidly had sex with him?'

Marybeth looked shocked—probably because Emily was never usually that frank. Or maybe it was because she'd lived like a nun for so long that her partner thought she was still a virgin.

'Is that what happened?' Marybeth questioned. 'I mean, I guessed there had been someone.'

Emily blinked. 'You did?'

Marybeth shrugged. 'Of course. You're lovely,' she said gently. 'But you always clammed up when it came to talking about men and then this really sad look would come over your face, so I didn't like to pry. And whenever you've dated anyone—which doesn't

happen often—nobody has come close to cap-
turing your heart, which suggested it must
have been badly broken. Is that what happened,
Em—with this guy Sabato? Did he break your
heart?'

Emily hesitated as she folded another cotton
shirt before adding it to the neat and sensible
pile already in her suitcase. She never talked
about it because it still had the power to hurt
and also because she was aware of how badly
she'd handled it—in fact, she couldn't have
handled it more badly if she'd tried. But maybe
she should talk about it. Maybe she needed to
make sense of it in her own head, so that she
could deal with it competently when she came
into contact with him again. 'Alejandro was
the housekeeper's son when I lived in Argentina,' she began slowly. 'In the days when my
mother was married to Paul Vickery.'

'That's the guy who left you the horse?'

Emily nodded. 'That's the one. Cruel and
calculating, but ultimately very rich—at
least, he was when I was a child. My mother
was completely in thrall to him, mainly because he'd rescued her from a life of poverty
as a widow. My father was a fisherman who
drowned off the Cornish coast, but even when
he was alive, money was scarce. After he died

my mother met Paul and felt as if she'd hit the jackpot. She'd found herself a rich husband who gave her a financial security she didn't have to work for. It's one of the reasons why my career has always been so important to me. Why I've been determined never to rely on a man like that.'

She heaved out a sigh. 'And even though he was chronically unfaithful, Paul only had to snap his fingers and she came running, which is what rich men really want women to do— and then they despise them for it. He had a thing about status. A big thing. Socialising in the highest echelons of society was his bag and his stepdaughter mixing with the illegitimate son of the hired help certainly didn't fit into that image, despite the fact that Alej was clearly going to be a big star in the world of polo. It may have been even more basic than that. Alejandro was at his physical peak and poised on the cusp of glory and my stepfather was getting very old by then—so maybe it was that old lion, young lion thing. When he found out I was involved with Alej, he demanded I finish it.'

'So you did?'

It sounded weak to admit it now, but, yes, she'd caved in and done exactly as her stepfather had demanded—mainly because her mother had got down on her knees in that over-the-top way of hers and begged her to. Had sobbed that Paul would never forgive her if she didn't and she couldn't cope with a divorce and going back to being a single mother. The ensuing drama had felt like an embarrassing nightmare and in the end Emily had agreed. But she'd convinced herself it was all for the best and it would save her even more heart-break further on down the line, because surely to Alej she was nothing more than a brief fling. A teenage love affair which wasn't going any-where—especially when increasing numbers of women were lining up beside the polo pitch to watch him play and making their availability very plain. Just as she'd told herself she would soon forget him. That the latter part of her as-sessment had never come true wasn't anyone's fault, particularly not his.

'Yes,' she said. 'I finished it.'

I finished it in the most horrible way pos-sible which still makes me shudder to think about it, which is why I rarely do.

'So why do you think he's chosen you to salvage his image, out of all the PR represen-tatives in the world?' questioned Marybeth slowly.

'He says he wants to go into politics,' Emily answered, her brow furrowing into a thoughtful frown. 'And needs to shed his bad-boy reputation pretty sharpish.'

'And that's it?' Marybeth's eyes glinted. 'That's the only reason he's employing you?'

It was a question Emily didn't want to answer as she snapped her suitcase closed and gave Marybeth a bright smile. 'I guess so. What other reason could there be?'

But she thought about her partner's question all the way to Heathrow airport and through the long flight which followed, which was delayed further by a technical problem on the plane which was supposed to take them from Brunei to Melbourne. Hadn't there been a whisper of revenge underpinning the dogmatic way Alejandro had demanded she go and work for him? Was the unspoken clause that he wanted to capitalise on the undoubted chemistry which still existed between them, or was that just her imagination? Because that was never going to happen, no matter what the provocation. No matter that she still found him the sexiest man she'd ever set eyes on, she wasn't going to tumble into his arms the way she used to do. She didn't dare. Why would she put herself through something like that when

the cold glint in Alejandro's eyes made no secret of the fact that he now despised her? All
she needed to do was to resurrect his battered
public image and earn the money he had promised her. Simple.

It was hot when she arrived in Melbourne—
hotter than Emily had expected, though she'd
never been to Australia before. She felt grimy
and sticky after the long journey but was due
to meet Alejandro at the racetrack and reck-
oned a trip to her hotel to freshen up would
make her even later than she already was. So
she scurried into a washroom at the airport
and did the best she could in the cramped surroundings, but the creases in the clean dress
she pulled on were stubbornly refusing to fall
out and her cheeks were flushed and shiny.

Passing a news stand, she saw Alejandro's
rugged features staring back from the front
page of a tabloid underneath the headline *Billionaire's Racy Race Party!*

Digging into her purse for some coins, she
tucked the newspaper into her bag and read it
during the bus ride to the stadium, hating the
way her heart sank as she pored over the feature, thinking how much one of the women
photographed entering his hotel resembled his

ex-mistress—a fact which hadn't escaped the notice of the journalist. It gave them the perfect opportunity to print an old picture of Colette and Alejandro kissing passionately at the Monaco Grand Prix and Emily couldn't rid herself of the image of the supermodel's long fingers splayed possessively over the Argentinian billionaire's taut bottom.

She was still feeling peculiar when the bus arrived at the race venue in Albert Park, and the constant droning of powerful cars coming from inside the stadium only added to her feelings of disorientation. Her phone started vibrating and she didn't need to see the name to know who it was from, as she squinted at it in the sunshine. The terse message blazing from the screen could have originated from only one person.

Where the hell are you?

Alejandro. Sounding angry and impatient. Was this going to be his default mechanism with her from now on? she wondered. But at least he'd kept his side of the bargain and, just before she'd left England, a batch of photos had arrived, each showing Joya. Now happily rehomed in Alejandro's vast Argentinian ranch, the horse's body had started to fill out and gleam with health as he stood regarding the camera with some of his perky expression of old. Unexpected tears had pricked at Emily's eyes as she'd stared at the images and she'd felt an overwhelming burst of gratitude as she'd boarded the night bus to the airport.

And now it was time for her to keep *her* side of the bargain, despite her misgivings.

She tapped out a reply.

Yes, I had a very pleasant trip—thanks for asking!

Another terse reply shot straight back.

Where are you?

This was going to be fun, thought Emily as her fingers flew over the smooth surface of the screen.

Just going up to the VIP section as instructed. Assume someone will meet me there?

There was no response to this one, so she picked up her suitcase and asked for directions, before heading for the gate where a small but well-heeled throng were congregated. Emily looked around with interest, because she'd never been to a motor-racing event before and it was a lot dressier than she'd imagined. Some of the women were wearing expensive skinny jeans and floaty blouses with discreet diamonds glinting at their ears and wrists, while others were in silk dresses with crazy-high heels. Emily frowned. Maybe Marybeth had been right in insisting that she borrow some fancy clothes for the trip, after all. Surreptitiously, she smoothed down her hair, uncomfortably aware that her battered suitcase was standing out like a sore thumb amid all the soft designer handbags.

Everyone was being ushered through the metal turnstile without fanfare, but as soon as Emily stepped forward, a burly security guard planted himself in front of her.

'Pass?' he said, extending the palm of his hand.

'I should have been left one at the gate.' Emily forced a smile, acutely aware of the beads of sweat which were springing up on her forehead and of a woman in front who had turned round to give her a haughty look. She wanted to exude her usual air of competence but for some reason it seemed to be eluding her. 'By Alejandro Sabato.'

The security man raised his eyebrows. 'Alejandro Sabato? The sponsor?'

'That's right. He's expecting me.'

'Is he now?' The guard could barely keep the smirk from his lips. 'That's what they all say, love. I'm afraid it's more than my job's worth to let you in without a ticket.'

'It's okay, Wesley.' A rich, accented voice filtered through the warm air towards them. 'I can vouch for her.'

The guard's demeanour quickly changed to one of near adulation as Alejandro came through the turnstile, irritation hardening the perfection of his olive-skinned features as he strode towards them. With an impatient movement he gestured for her to move away and Emily was glad to remove herself from the glances they were attracting. Were people bemused by how mismatched the two of them looked? Mightn't she have thought exactly the same if she'd been the outsider?

She wished she could slow down the racing of her heart, just as she wished she could stop her body from prickling with instinctive hunger as she surveyed the man towering over her, with anger glinting from his green eyes. Today he was dressed down in faded denims and a creamy silk shirt, but his casual clothes didn't detract from the unmistakable air of authority and power which radiated from his body. Dark waves of hair were curling onto the collar of his shirt, their unruly profusion somehow at odds with his upright stance and the perfect posture which had always been remarked upon during his riding career. People were taking sneaky photos of him with their phones but he didn't appear to notice.

'You're late,' he accused, as soon as they were out of earshot.

'I know. Sorry about that. It couldn't be helped.'

'Why not? What happened?' he demanded. 'Was the plane delayed?'

'Sort of. There was a tech problem.' Emily shifted the strap of her shoulder bag to stop it rubbing. 'Which delayed the second flight, so the journey took longer than the twenty-eight hours it was supposed to take.'

'More than twenty-eight hours?' he echoed incredulously. 'How is that even possible?'

She wondered if he'd forgotten what it was like to be poor, or to be starting out. If he knew what it was like to consult comparison sites on the web before you took a plane anywhere—or whether he was so used to travelling around in private jets and helicopters that such a mode of transport now seemed completely normal to him. 'I bought the cheapest ticket available, which meant it took a somewhat…um…' she gave a sheepish shrug '…indirect route.'

His eyes narrowed. 'Even though you had a budget which allowed you to travel first class, which I believe was agreed in advance with my assistant?'

'That's right.'

'So?' His eyes bored into her questioningly.

'So I couldn't justify spending that kind of money on a plane ticket and flying to the other side of the world in the lap of luxury, Alejandro. Not when my business is in such a fledgling state and we're still having to budget like crazy because most people don't pay on time. Every penny counts at this stage—that's why we're careful.' She hesitated, and then a smile seemed to spring out of nowhere as she looked at him with gratitude. 'But I wanted to thank you for everything you've done for Joya. He seems so happy now and those pictures of him at your ranch look amazing.'

'It's called an *estancia*,' he snapped.

'Whatever.' Her smile widened. 'But thanks, anyway.'

Alejandro wanted to hang onto his anger but when she looked at him like that it wasn't easy, and it was causing his conscience to stir in an uncharacteristic way, because she looked so damned sweet. But she wasn't sweet, he reminded himself grimly. She was as money-grabbing as her mother. And she was a heartless snob. When she'd walked away from him, she had looked down her pretty nose and given him a shuttered look when he'd asked her why.

You're not the right type of man for me, Alej.

He hadn't known what she'd meant, not at first. He'd been rough and unsophisticated back then. He'd seen the uncomfortable look which had crossed her features. The way she'd licked her lips, like someone being forced to eat cat food. Like a fool he had asked her, unable to believe that Emily—his Emily—could look at him so condescendingly, as if she'd never met him before.

You're illegitimate.

And that matters? he remembered demanding incredulously.

It matters to me.

He'd wanted to tell her that his mother might not wear a wedding ring on her finger, but that his father was someone whose wealth and position could easily eclipse that of her stepfather. But he hadn't done that, because at heart Alejandro Sabato was a proud man. And, in view of what had subsequently happened, thank God he hadn't.

But dwelling on his hurt and his anger wasn't going to get him anywhere—at least, not at this precise moment. Instead, Alejandro pushed away the ugly thoughts as he raked his gaze over her. He had wondered if the intervening years might have given her an air of sophistication, but they certainly hadn't. At the ranch she could have been excused for her plain jeans and T-shirt—but in the VIP section of one of the world's most prestigious race events, she could not.

His mouth thinned into a disapproving line, for he had imagined she would make herself beautiful for him, as women always did. He wondered if this was some kind of subtle rebellion—turning up with her face bare of makeup and wearing a cheap cotton dress. And why was her blonde hair hanging over one shoulder in that thick and wholesome plait, so she looked like some superannuated milkmaid rather than a smooth PR he'd hired to revamp his playboy image?

Yet her drab clothes were doing nothing to dampen his ardour for her. If anything, her prim outfit was heating his blood with a passion he hadn't felt in years and he was having difficulty averting his gaze from her luscious curves, which no plain shift dress could possibly disguise. His throat dried. He resented the physical allure she still seemed to radiate, despite her second-rate appearance. Was she aware that the thin material was brushing tantalisingly against her generous breasts, reminding him all too vividly of the way he used to stroke them until she moaned? Or that her bare legs were making his groin grow exquisitely hard as he wondered what type of panties she was wearing and was filled with a sudden overwhelming desire to discover the answer for himself. Later, he promised himself, with a fierce beat of hunger. Later.

Deliberately, he swivelled his gaze away from her, directing it instead towards the battered suitcase she was clutching. 'And *that*?' he demanded, with soft incredulity.

'It's my suitcase. Obviously.' She tilted a defiant chin. 'I didn't want to be any later than I already was, so I came straight here without checking into my hotel first.'

'Well, you can't stay here, not looking like that.' He fished a shoal of car keys from the back pocket of his jeans and took the case from her. 'My car isn't far away. I'll take you to your hotel so you can change. Or at least iron your dress.'

'I'm very grateful for the sartorial tips, Alejandro. Perhaps you'd like to colour-coordinate my wardrobe for me while I'm here?'

Ignoring her sarcastic comments, he glanced at his gold watch. 'The qualifying session is over and the main race isn't until tomorrow. There's a party on a yacht down in the harbour I need to attend, but that's not until later. Come on. Don't let's waste any more time. Let's go.'

He was so…*bossy*, Emily thought, and part of her wanted to object to his high-handedness. To tell him she'd prefer to start working straight away and check into her hotel later, but that would have been a lie. To be honest, she didn't think she could concentrate on anything right now, especially not on the closely written notes she'd made when he'd first given her the contract. Her brain felt fuzzy and her limbs were as heavy as lead, after being stuck in the middle row of a crowded plane between two women, one of whom had crunched on boiled sweets for the entire flight. Hopefully a quick shower and change of clothes would turn her back into her usual efficient self.

Because she was *good* at her job, she reminded herself fiercely. That was why she and Marybeth had taken the decision to leave the big agency they'd been working at and go it alone. She might be a complete disaster where relationships were concerned, but at least her career was going somewhere. And this was the chance to prove it—to herself and to the world at large. Because if she could single-handedly turn around Alejandro Sabato's bad-boy image, wouldn't that bring in a whole stream of new contracts and catapult their company onto the next level? Wasn't that what she'd been striving for all these years?

So she nodded and smiled at him. 'Okay,' she said politely. 'That'd be good.'

It felt weird having someone carry her bag for her. She'd been on her own for so long that it seemed like a luxury—and a poignant one at that. But deep down she knew it didn't mean anything. Outwardly Alejandro might be acting like a gentleman but there was no denying his underlying hostility towards her, which no acts of chivalry could disguise.

They made their way to a car park, where mouth-wateringly expensive vehicles were sitting in gleaming rows. Slinging her suitcase into the boot of one of the most luxurious, he punched out the postcode she'd given him and powered the car out of the park like a restless animal which had just been released for the day.

It quickly became clear that he was driving in an unfamiliar part of the city because he cursed several times in Spanish as they drove past a series of giant business parks before reaching a downmarket residential area, where graffiti was daubed on boarded-up shop windows and litter drifted in slow motion through the streets. Although a relatively short distance away from the racetrack, it seemed like a world away from all the glitz and glamour Emily had glimpsed there. As he pulled upside a motel with dirty windows and two letters missing from the sign, she saw him scowl before slamming his fist against the steering wheel and turning to look at her, undisguised irritation darkening his rugged features.

'Don't tell me,' he said. 'This was the cheapest hotel you could find?'

'Actually, it's five-star—just very cunningly disguised.'

'Cut the sarcasm, Emily,' he snapped, before twisting the key in the ignition again so that the engine powered into renewed life. 'You're not staying here.'

'That's just where you're wrong, Alejandro.

I am. This is where I've booked to stay and my room is paid for in advance. I'm perfectly prepared to rough it for a few days and my accommodation is my concern, not yours.' She put her fingers on the door handle. 'Besides, I don't have anywhere else to go.'

'Yes, you do. Don't you dare move. You're not going anywhere.' His no-nonsense tone brooked no argument as he turned the car back towards the city.

'What are you doing?'

'Taking you somewhere which will have easy access to the race ground.'

'I'm not spending all my budget on a fancy hotel—'

'Let me worry about the budget, Emily. Just sit back and enjoy the ride.'

Enjoy the ride? He was *definitely* crazy. Yet somehow…somehow… Emily found herself doing exactly that. She blamed the accumulated jet lag of recent back-to-back flights across the globe for her compliance, because why else would she have settled back into the squishy comfort of the seat, secretly relieved not to have to stay in that ghastly motel, which looked nothing like it had done on the website?

And wasn't she secretly enjoying watching Alej manoeuvre the powerful car through the city streets? It felt like something of a voyeuristic and guilty distraction to observe the thrust of his muscular thighs as he deftly weaved in and out of traffic, and before long he was drawing up outside a beautiful hotel in the historic part of the city. Ornate spires soared up into a cloudless blue sky and window boxes of bright pink flowers added splashes of colour to the gracious façade. Emily glanced up at the sign. Even if her research hadn't flagged up this as one of the most exclusive places to stay in the city—she could have worked that out for herself.

'No way. I can't possibly stay here,' she objected. 'This is one of the best hotels in Melbourne.'

'You have no choice. Everywhere else will be full because of the race.' His voice was underpinned with the steely certainty that here was a man used to getting everything he wanted. 'I have a suite. There's plenty of room. Don't worry, Emily—there's no cause for concern.'

No cause for concern? A low laugh punched its way out of Emily's lungs as she stared at his olive-skinned profile, where once she used to run a gentle fingertip along the shadowed edge of his jutting jaw. Had he become the master of understatement in the intervening years or was he just oblivious to the glaringly obvious? 'You really think I'm going to share a suite with you?'

'What's the problem?' He turned his head to look at her, his green eyes hard and flinty. 'I know we never made it to the hotel stage in our relationship but surely you've shared accommodation with a man before. And most women manage to rent in mixed houses these days, don't they—without it resulting in some kind of orgy?'

'But we've—'

'Had sex?' he supplied baldly. 'Yeah, in theory we did. Though in reality it was just plenty of foreplay and a single night of romping amid bales of straw before you ran out on me next morning, which hardly qualifies for the deepest and most meaningful relationship of all time. Unless you think I won't be able to stop myself from leaping on you because you're just so damned alluring?'

As he spoke, his gaze was raking over her with undeniable mockery and suddenly Emily felt foolish in her cheap dress and flat sandals. 'I wasn't implying—'

'Yes, you were.' His voice lowered. 'Believe me, Emily—I prefer women who take a little more care with their appearance than you do.

But most of all, I like them willing. You, of all people, should know that.'

She could feel her flush deepening and the palms of her hands growing even clammier as she wiped them down the sides of her dress. It was an unkind and unnecessary comment to make. But it was true, wasn't it? She had made it clear that she'd been his for the taking when she'd fallen in love with him. He'd been six years older and had tried to do the honourable thing, but that hadn't deterred her. At the age of seventeen it was as if all the scales had fallen from her eyes. Overnight, it seemed, their platonic friendship had changed and she had looked at him with a hunger she hadn't known before, or since. She had been ready, willing and available whenever the opportunity had arisen. All those snatched and stolen moments had only added an extra layer of excitement to their secret relationship. And then, when he had given her what she'd wanted, she had walked away with nothing but a few cruel words lingering in her wake.

She had done it because she'd been backed into a corner by her stepfather, who had made all kinds of horrible threats.

But hadn't a tiny part of her been relieved to walk away? To be free of all that compulsion

*and desire and obsession, which had made her
fear she was too much like her foolish mother?
That she would end up becoming weak and dependent on a man?*

'There are two bedrooms,' Alejandro was
saying. 'You can have your own space if that's
what you want—'

'Of course it's what I want,' she snapped.
'Surely you don't think I'm sharing a room
with you?'

'It would be a novel experience,' he observed
softly. 'And one I'd be willing to try.'

'In your dreams,' she retorted as a valet approached to open the door for her.

'Yours too, perhaps?' he suggested, with a
pointed glance at her hardening nipples.

'Will you please stop making innuendos?'

'I'm not.' He slanted her a mocking smile.
'I'm merely making an observation.'

Pre-empting the approaching valet, Emily
opened the car door herself, furious at the ac-
curacy of Alejandro's arrogant words but even
more furious at the way she couldn't seem to
help her body from responding to him. Suddenly she was aware of a rush of heat which
pooled at her groin, but most of all she was
aware of the Argentinian's appreciative gaze
on her bare legs as she wriggled out of the car.

CHAPTER FOUR

'It's him! It's definitely him! Hey, Alej—can we get a selfie with you?'

Two beautiful young American women with tumbling hair and super-tight denim shorts had spotted their entry into the hotel and were clattering their way across the lobby towards them on gravity-defying shoes.

'No,' snapped Emily. 'Refuse politely.'

Alejandro turned his head towards her, his dark brows raised. 'Why?'

'Because if you're serious about politics, you need to stop people constantly seeing you with gorgeous women fawning all over you. It makes you look like a lightweight and a flirt. Tell them you're expecting a call.'

'But I'm not.'

'Just make an excuse.'

'If you insist,' he said drily.

'I do. And my advice is what you're paying for. Remember?'

'When did you get so insistent, Emily?'

'When I started my own business and rec-ognised the need to assert myself. It's a par-ticularly useful trait when I'm dealing with stubborn men.'

'You don't say?' he mocked.

'Indeed, I do. Now, be polite by all means—if such a concept isn't alien to you—but walk straight past them.'

Without pausing mid-stride, Alejandro called out his apologies to the two women, who pouted prettily as he and Emily made their way towards the elevator. She wondered if she had imagined their look of astonishment as they'd stared at the Argentinian's companion but an unexpected glimpse of herself as they walked past an enormous rose-gold mirror made her realise just how awful she looked.

The doors of the executive elevator slid open and the rapid ride towards the penthouse was just long enough to remind her what real lux-ury felt like. She hadn't experienced it since her mother's marriage to Paul, when extrav-agance had been part of her daily life and it had been drummed into her that she must be grateful at all times. Grateful that her stepfa-ther had given her a home—and what a home!

And she had tried. She'd tried so hard. Pre-tended not to mind those interminable dinners, which had gone on and on and the adults had forgotten she was there. Pretended not to be bored at being dragged around yet another stuffy museum to which her stepfather had donated money in his attempt to ingratiate himself into society. Because wasn't all that preferable to listening to the muffled sobs of her mother and having to play ignorant about where she'd left her bottle of pills?

Sometimes it seemed she'd spent her whole life pretending. She was even pretending now, wasn't she? Trying to make out that she wasn't in the least bit affected by the sexy hunk who was standing on the other side of the elevator.

'We're here.' Alejandro's words shattered her reverie and Emily followed him into an enormous suite where the first thing she saw— perched on a raised dais—was a white baby grand piano.

Searching round for evidence of more luxury, she quickly found it. Futuristic glass lights in candy shades spilled shafts of colours all over the modern, monochrome furniture. An angular sculpture stood framed against the city sky in one of the vast picture windows. Everything seemed so stark and pristine, which somehow emphasised Alejandro's earthy appeal as he put down her suitcase and walked towards a large desk. His olive skin glowed as he glanced down at a pile of cards and began to flick his way through them. The thick tumble of his hair looked almost blue-black in the sunshine and suddenly Emily found herself wanting to run her fingers through the lustrous waves, just like in the old days. She wanted to press her body up against his and slide her tongue against the roughness of his shadowed jaw. And yet it was dangerous to feel like that. She might be unfulfilled, but at least she was not hung up and obsessing. Not bereft or aching or staring at her phone, waiting for some man who was never going to ring.

She thought how at home he seemed in this lavish setting, he who had been born to abject poverty—and how, ironically, it was her who now felt out of place. And her travel-weary and un-showered state wasn't exactly helping. How could she possibly concentrate on work when she still felt so hot and sticky—especially when Alejandro looked so cool and pristine?

'Perhaps you'd like to point me in the direction of my room?' she suggested. 'I'd like to freshen up before we get down to work.'

'Sure.' He picked up her suitcase. 'Come with me,' he said, observing her instinctively shrinking away as he came close.

Leading her down the wide and spacious corridor towards the two bedrooms, Alejandro wondered when she had become so uptight. He remembered her astride a horse, with the wind in her hair—someone who bore no resemblance to the sensible creature she'd become in her plain clothes. Maybe that was what happened to women when they lost their innocence. Perhaps they lost their softness, too. She was the only virgin he'd ever had so he had nobody to compare her with. Cynically, his mouth twisted. There weren't too many virgins to be found in the world he inhabited.

Flinging open a bedroom door where creamy drapes framed a blue sky, he wished he could just tumble her down on that big white bed and take her without ceremony. Because wouldn't some perfunctory sex rid his mind and body of his damned hunger for her?

'This is it.'

'Wow,' she said softly, glancing at the modern artwork which adorned the walls and appearing to look at everything in the room, except for the bed. She walked over to the window. 'That's some view.'

'Best in the city. Come and find me when

you've finished. And don't be long. There's a party on Marcus Hedlund's yacht in the harbour.'

'The Swedish industrialist?'

'The very same. I hope you've come suitably prepared.' His gaze swept over the wilting fabric of her dress. 'These affairs tend to be quite dressy.'

'I know that. I've done my research. Don't worry, Alejandro. I'll try not to let you down.'

The quick tilt of her chin suddenly reminded Alejandro of the daredevil teenager he'd once taught to ride and something unknown and dark twisted deep inside him as he remembered how close they'd once been. Until he reminded himself that the teenager had grown up and become a snobbish replica of her grasping mother. 'I look forward to seeing what miracles you can perform,' he said curtly, before turning away.

Returning to the drawing room, he tried to concentrate on the pile of paperwork awaiting him, but for once he found it impossible to lose himself in his workload. He should have been overjoyed at the fact that he was about to float his highly successful drinks company on the stock market for an eye-watering sum of money. Whoever would have thought that every teenager on the planet would have considered it the height of cool to quaff a cleverly marketed drink which was packed with herbs from his homeland and based on Argentina's favourite drink of *yerba maté*? Or that every business gamble he'd ever taken would confound even his own expectations and lead him to unimaginable riches?

And all this had happened to someone who'd been born in a *villa miseria*—a miserable shack crammed beside hundreds of others in a dirty settlement outside Buenos Aires, with unpaved roads and no sanitation. Even after his mother had managed to shed her past for long enough to get herself a job as a rich Englishman's housekeeper, Alej's education had been almost non-existent. His passion and talent for riding had allowed him to put learning on the back burner and nobody had really cared that he'd skipped school most days. Able to read and write but without a single exam to his name, it had been a matter of pride and perseverance which had later made him devour books and newspapers and educate himself that way.

But his subsequent successes had never managed to fill the void deep inside him, or to lighten the darkness which seemed a fundamental part of his nature. He had been betrayed, first by Emily and then by his mother, and had sometimes wondered if those two key events had scarred him irrevocably, making him the man he had become—someone who functioned efficiently on every level but who never really *felt* anything. He would never know and he didn't really care. His mother was dead now, taking her sordid past to the grave with her, and he had tried with varying degrees of success not to be judgemental about the things she had done.

But Emily was alive, wasn't she? Delicious and luscious and *alive*. Some people said that moving into the future was only possible if you were properly reconciled with your past, and that was something which had so far eluded him. Until now. His mouth tightened. Because that was what he intended to do. To claim her. To enjoy her in a way which had not been possible before. To tie up all the loose ends so there was no chance they could ever become unravelled again.

The sound of soft footsteps broke into his thoughts and he looked up, his groin hardening when he saw Emily standing in the doorway.

He swallowed. A quick glance at his watch showed him that in a little over half an hour she had managed to achieve a remarkable transformation. Her newly washed hair had been piled into a messy updo which gave her a tantalising just-got-out-of-bed look. Escaping strands had already begun to dry dark gold and shiny as they tumbled around her long neck and framed a face which had been delicately touched with make-up.

But it was her outfit which made the most startling difference. Gone was the functional cotton shift and in its place a flirty dress of red silk, a colour he'd never seen her wear before. His throat tightened. Had she deliberately bought it a little on the small side, or was the delicate material supposed to cling to her generous breasts like that, so that he could barely tear his gaze away from them? Bright and bold, it had tiny buttons all the way down the front and fell to just above each shapely knee. Hugging her narrow waist, it flared slightly over her hips and the hot-faced, crumpled creature who had greeted him at the racetrack suddenly became a distant memory.

Alejandro couldn't fault the way she looked and yet something raw and primitive began to throb through his veins as he wondered how many times she had performed this Cinderella scenario in the past. Had she dressed up like this for other men? he thought, with a sharp surge of jealousy. Had they too been busy thinking about how much they'd like to slide their fingers beneath that scarlet hemline to caress her cool thighs, before travelling further upwards to find her melting wetness? A pulse throbbed at his temple. Of course they had. Why wouldn't they, when she'd been the hottest woman he had ever known and had told him that she planned to take as many lovers as possible? That declaration had filled him with an impotent rage for a long time after she'd left and he'd sometimes found himself punching at his pillow in the middle of the night, until he had completely flattened it.

But he doubted any man had pleasured Emily Green as thoroughly as he was about to do. He wanted to rip the dress from her body and for her panties to follow, but he forced himself to put his desire on ice and to adopt the indifferent mask which both intrigued and infuriated his many lovers.

'Did somebody wave a magic wand?' he questioned carelessly. 'Does it turn back into a sensible cotton dress at midnight?'

She gave a shrug which didn't quite come off. 'If you're referring to my outfit, I borrowed it from my friend, since she goes to a lot more fancy functions than I do.'

Which might explain why the dress was straining so tantalisingly across her breasts that he could see the faint outline of her nipples. He swallowed. 'I see.'

'But we aren't here to discuss my wardrobe choices,' she said, primly nodding her head like a schoolteacher who was about to start a lesson. 'I suggest we get down to work.'

'Of course,' he said. 'Though you could probably use a drink first?'

'Nothing alcoholic!' she responded swiftly.

He gave a low laugh. 'Don't worry, Emily. I wasn't planning on plying you with fine wine. I was offering you water.'

'Oh, right,' she said. 'Well, thanks. Water would be great.'

Emily watched as he got up from the desk, unable to tear her eyes away from him. She'd told him that she wanted to work, but the sight of Alejandro moving across the room made it difficult to concentrate on anything other than his dark beauty and physical grace, as he walked over to a sleek bar of polished black wood. He added ice to two drinks—yet when he handed her a glass it wasn't coldness she felt but a sizzle of fire as his skin brushed against hers.

She wondered what was the matter with her.

wrote—on your recommendation, I might add. According to her, you're very fond of these kinds of parties. And of the type of women who frequent them, often without invitation.'

'And you believed every word of it, I suppose—along with the rest of the world?' His face grew hard and assumed a look of unfettered cynicism. 'Especially the part where she hinted about me enjoying "variety"—which seemed to be the phrase which got most people excited. She made me sound like the worst kind of serial philanderer. She didn't actually mention mirrors on the ceiling and black satin sheets but she might as well have done—although, unfortunately, my lawyers told me there was nothing you could actually put your finger on and call libel.'

'And did you?'

'Did I what, Emily?' he mocked.

'Enjoy…' she licked her lips, wishing she could clear her thoughts of the image of Alejandro making out beneath a mirrored ceiling amid rumpled black satin sheets '…variety?'

'Never.' A note of contempt hardened his voice, matching the sudden forbidding line of his lips. 'I've always enjoyed the attentions of women, but only ever one at a time. And I've never found promiscuity a particularly

She didn't usually have showers which turned into something disturbingly erotic, but that was what had just happened as she'd washed herself in the luxury bathroom. The warm water had failed to remove the prickle of goosebumps as she'd started imagining Alejandro's fingers sliding over her flesh and the corresponding throb of her nipples had made her feel restless as she had towelled herself dry. Yet this was *nothing like* the person she usually was. The prim and efficient woman she'd become. She prided herself on the professionalism which was so important to her and on her ability to think coolly and impartially. So stop focussing on sex and start concentrating on what you're being paid for, she reminded herself.

Sipping at her water, she cleared her throat and put the glass down. 'Right. First of all, I think we need to establish some clear objectives.'

'Some clear objectives?' he echoed, green eyes faintly mocking. 'Perhaps you could be a little more specific.'

'Certainly. We're going to use this high-profile weekend to make people start thinking about you in a different way. But in order for us to work together successfully, I need you to be completely frank with me. You have to answer my questions truthfully, Alejandro. Do you think you can do that?'

'I can try.' He stared at her. 'What exactly do you want to know?'

She jerked her head towards the white baby grand. 'Why the fancy piano?'

'Rock and roll,' he explained with a touch of bemusement, as if her question was a curveball he hadn't been expecting. 'The hotel send up a pianist if any of their guests want to hold an impromptu party.'

'Is that what happened last night?'

He raised his eyebrows. 'Last night?'

'Surely you can remember back to a few hours ago? You say you want to abandon your playboy image in order to pave the way for a possible career in politics, but you aren't exactly going out of your way to help yourself, are you?'

'I don't know what you're talking about.'

'This!' Emily delved deep within her shoulder bag to produce a folded newspaper, which she held in front of him, the splashy headline easily visible. 'I picked this up at the airport and it features a gushing report about the "wild, champagne-fuelled celebration" you held last night. There was even a photo of a very beautiful actress staggering out in the

early hours, obviously the worse for wear. If you're going to plan a party, I would advise you to think more carefully about your guest list in future.'

'I didn't plan a party, it just happened.' He shrugged as he met the question in her eyes. 'Two of the other sponsors wanted to see the view from my suite. It's a pretty amazing view—'

'I can see that for myself. Perhaps you could try sticking to the point? It will save us a lot of time if you do.'

He gave a slow smile in response to her sharp words, as if being admonished was something novel. 'And they brought a few people along with them. You know what it's like.'

'Not really, no.'

He seemed undeterred by her stonewalling. 'Apparently a few of the models who are in town for the race gatecrashed a bit later, but I'd gone to bed by then.'

'Alone?' she demanded quickly.

'That sounds like the accusation of a possessive girlfriend,' he observed softly. 'Or what a prosecution lawyer might call a very loaded question.'

'Or a pertinent one?' she returned. 'Just for the record, I read the book your ex-girlfriend

attractive quality. You of all people should know that.'

Emily flinched, wondering if he'd believed the stupid lie she'd told him. And why shouldn't he have believed it when she'd made it sound so convincing? Hadn't she practised saying it over and over again?

Alej, I don't want to be with you any more. I don't love you any more.

And then, when he had persisted, she had taken the lie one stage further.

It was only ever about sex and I've seen other men in England. Men who are more suitable. Rich, well-bred men I want more than you.

It had been so over the top that she'd half wondered if she'd gone too far and whether he would see through it for the invention it was. But he hadn't. He had believed every word of it and she would never forget the answering look in his eyes. Not for as long as she lived.

But there was a different look in his eyes now because while they'd been talking something had changed. His gaze was no longer icy-cold as it had been the day he'd touched down in his helicopter in Argentina, nor disapproving like when she'd arrived in Melbourne a couple of hours ago. Now it held some of the familiar heat of old as he looked at her, and some of the old hunger, too. It spoke to a feeling inside her. A feeling which had been dead for so long that she'd thought she'd lost it for ever. Or maybe it was just that only Alejandro could ignite it. Only he could make her body seem as if it had fired into vibrant new life.

Against the scarlet silk of her bodice she could feel the ripening thrust of her nipples and, low in her belly, the first sweet rush of awakening, and in those few seconds she longed for him to touch her again. To do those things which used to give her so much pleasure. Most of all, she wanted him to kiss her. To put his arms around her. To make her feel safe and protected.

And that was the feeling which scared her most of all, because you could never rely on a man to provide you with sanctuary. Hadn't that been just about the only thing her mother *had* taught her?

So concentrate, she urged herself fiercely. Don't start thinking like that, and don't start acting in a way which will lead you into trouble. Send out the subliminal message that this is strictly professional and if you start believing it yourself, then Alejandro might believe it, too.

'You're going to need to start protecting your own space a bit more in future,' she advised. 'You can't just let parties *happen*. If things get out of hand it's your image which will be damaged and you need to start guarding it more carefully. Image control, they call it.' She tucked a stray strand of hair behind her ear and subjected him to a cool look. 'We need the world to start thinking of you in a new way, so your reputation as a playboy becomes a thing of the past and in its place comes the sometimes serious, always thoughtful would-be politician.'

'But achieving that is going to be a monumental turnaround, I suppose?' he suggested sardonically.

'I'm not denying it's going to be a challenge, but I have a few ideas.' Feeling more confident now, Emily unzipped her shoulder bag and drew out a plastic-covered folder, keen to prove she'd done her homework. 'I understand your team is going to present you with a special award after tomorrow's race—as a thank-you for all your backing and support and for ploughing so much money into the sport. I think we can use that ceremony as a platform.'

He frowned. 'A platform for what?'

She drew in a deep breath. 'Tell me why you want to go into politics.'

A few seconds elapsed before he began to speak. 'I've been approached by the progressive new party which is riding high in the polls and they are keen for me to represent them. A breath of fresh air blowing through the stale air in the political arena is how they're terming my inclusion.'

'That's the method, Alejandro—not the reason. You haven't told me why you want to do it.'

Alejandro saw the scepticism in her gaze, slightly disconcerted by the thought that she might be more perceptive than he'd given her credit for. He felt a flicker of irritation. Did she see his ambition as nothing more than a stunt— the latest shiny hobby for a man who was bored with life? Was it that which made him want to demonstrate that there was more to him than the cliché? The daredevil sportsman turned billionaire playboy. The shallow, two-dimensional Lothario invented by the press. A wealthy man who cared for nothing but gambling and seduction and expensive toys. Because he was more than that. Much more.

And maybe because it was Emily, he found himself speaking with the kind of candour he might not have used with anyone else. Was that because once she had known him better than anyone? Before the helicopters and the private jets and the homes scattered carelessly around the globe?

'Because there are still people who are born poor and hungry, just as I was,' he husked. 'People condemned to a deprivation which will be repeated through every generation which follows—unless, like me, they're lucky enough to be born with a gift. People who die before their time because decent healthcare isn't available. I want to help to change that,' he finished. 'And politics is a route towards making that happen.'

'That's good. In fact, it's very good,' she commented slowly. 'I think you should say something on those lines when you accept your award tomorrow evening—especially if you can manage to replicate the same degree of passion and conviction.'

Alejandro heard the insinuation, which was highlighted by the look of surprise which had grown on her face while he'd been speaking. Was she suggesting his message was all about delivery, rather than content? That it was more style than substance? Did she believe in the cliché herself? His jaw tightened and suddenly he was angry with himself for caring *what* she thought. Because he didn't have anything to prove. Not to her—of all people.

'You think I'm just a showman, do you, Emily?' he murmured as, without warning, he reached out to cup her chin between his thumb and forefinger so that their gazes were locked on a collision course. That first contact felt like pure, powerful electricity and he waited, wondering if she would push him away. But she didn't. Of course she didn't. Because the chemistry between them hadn't changed, had it? She was as hot for him as she'd ever been. He could see it in the nipples which were thrusting like iron tips against the scarlet silk of her dress, and in the way her lips automatically parted. He had desired many women in his life but his lust for Emily seemed to be stamped into his very DNA and, even though he despaired of it, his blood was heating at the thought of what he was about to do. He stroked his finger slowly over her cheek. 'You think my words are empty?'

'I...' The word was breathless and the sapphire of her eyes nothing but thin rims against the fathomless black pooling. 'Alejandro... what...what are you doing?'

He could see the pulse which was hammering away beside an errant strand of blonde hair and already he could detect the faint perfume of her sex. If he'd been feeling stronger he might have denied her. Made her wait. Left her high and dry before going to relieve his own frustration, alone in his bedroom, in a way he hadn't done for years. Because wouldn't it make her even hotter if he spun it out? But he couldn't. How could he, when his groin was on fire? When the hard bulge pressing so exquisitely against his jeans felt as if it might explode at any moment?

'Let's pass on the game-playing, shall we, Emily? I'm about to do exactly what you want me to do,' he said, his throat thick and tight. 'In fact, it's the only thing you've ever really wanted me to do, because I sure as hell was never good enough for anything else.'

Emily saw his head lowering towards her in slow motion, giving her all the time in the world to stop him. But she didn't. How could she, when most of what he said was true? Because yes, she wanted him. She'd never really stopped wanting him—not through all the arid years since last he'd held her like this. Because Alejandro Sabato possessed a power which he wielded over her like some dark and erotic spell. He could make her hot for him. Wet for him. Instantly.

She shuddered when at last he bent his head to kiss her because it had been a long time since anyone had kissed her, and never like this. Only Alej could kiss like this. His tongue slid inside her mouth and the intimacy of that fed her spiralling hunger as she looped her arms around his neck. And then she was close. Close enough to feel the sudden hard jerk of his erection pressing against her.

'Alej,' she whispered against his mouth and this time he didn't object to the familiar use of his name.

His response was to stroke his fingertip down her neck, drifting a slow line to her cleavage—before slipping it inside her dress to cup her straining breast. And still she didn't object. How could she, when he was tracing a tantalising circle over one rock-hard nipple which was thrusting eagerly against his finger? He deepened the kiss and she writhed against him. Hungrily. Restlessly. And then, without warning, he scooped her up into his arms and carried her over to a huge black leather sofa before depositing her on top of it. She was on *fire*…so eager for him to touch her again that she didn't care about the implications of being horizontal. All she could think about was how much she wanted him in her arms and she groaned with pleasure as he lay down on top of her, his mouth reclaiming hers with an urgency as flattering as it was irresistible.

Her eyes closed as she gave herself up to sensation and suddenly it was nothing *but* sensation.

The honeyed beat of blood in her veins.

The throbbing heat between her legs and exquisite peaking of her breasts.

'Mmm…' he said as he continued his expert caress of one puckered nipple, through her bra. 'I had forgotten just how delicious these were and now I want to see them again for myself.'

Each word was punctuated by the swift undoing of each tiny button, his fingers operating with a dexterity which spoke of vast experience. And even though that should have daunted her, Emily felt powerless to protest—especially when the air felt so deliciously cool against her heated skin. Or maybe it was because he forestalled any such protest by the highly effective method of using his other hand to inch up beneath the hemline of her dress. The breath shuddered from her lungs. It had been eight years since anyone had touched her like this and it felt as if she had tumbled into paradise.

But he seemed momentarily surprised as

the sides of her dress flapped open to reveal her bra.

'Oh, my,' he breathed.

'Is something wrong?' she questioned dazedly, opening her eyes to see him studying her breasts with rapt attention.

He shrugged as he tested the elastic of one flesh-coloured strap and it pinged rather inefficiently against her skin. 'This doesn't exactly fulfil the promise of the sexy dress.'

That was definite censure she could hear in his voice. Was he criticising the T-shirt bra she wore beneath all her clothes to give her a smooth line as well as contain her too-large breasts? 'It's practical,' she defended.

'I'm sure it is. It is also a little plain.' He gave a lazy smile as he resumed his teasing ministrations. 'Don't the other men in your life demand you wear pretty lingerie from time to time?'

'What other men?' she supplied, her overstimulated body playing havoc with her thought processes, especially when he was stroking her nipple like that.

'I'm not going to flatter myself I'm the only one, particularly after your parting words to me,' he whispered against her neck. 'Or is your air of gauche innocence just a perk you provide to all your clients?'

It took a few moments for his meaning to register and when it did, the implication was so insulting that it completely took her breath away. 'A *perk*?'

He shrugged. 'Why not? It happens.'

Emily stared at him incredulously before pushing his hand away and slithering out from beneath him to scramble to her feet. Her hands were shaking with rage as she tugged the flapping halves of her dress together and began to rebutton it, glaring at him where he lay, like some dark and indolent panther. 'You really think I would behave like that with just…*anyone*? That I would do this kind of thing with *clients*?'

Unperturbed by her accusation, he got up, raking his fingers back through the tumble of his hair, before tugging down his shirt and tucking it into his jeans. 'I don't know,' he said coldly. 'Discrimination was never your strong point, Emily. When you left you told me you were going to enjoy other men and I'm assuming you did.'

Because it had been the only way she could ensure he would let her go. The only way she could guarantee he wouldn't test her resolve.

But what was the point of raking all that up now and revisiting a past which was surely best left forgotten? Even if he *was* looking at her as if she were nothing but a cheap tramp who put out for anyone who happened to turn her on. She wasn't here to parade her virtue or seek his good opinion of her. And wouldn't it make it easier to deal with the attraction which still burned between them if on one level he continued to despise her? She smoothed her dress down over her hips, and only when she was confident that her image was restored did she lift her gaze to his.

'I'm not quite sure how that happened,' she said, in a voice which sounded unnaturally calm.

'You want me to describe for you how hormones work?' he drawled.

Ignoring his sarcasm, Emily made her voice sound bright, like the one she'd used all those times when she'd been trying to rouse her mother from the deepest of sleeps. It was a note of determination, but it was also one of survival. Even if it didn't always work—you still had to give it a try. 'And we're going to forget that it ever did happen. Do you understand that, Alejandro?'

He gave a low laugh. 'Oh, I understand more than you think, *querida*, but I'm afraid it's not that easy. Because you want me, Emily. You might wish you didn't, but you do. You want me so badly I can almost *taste* it and, beneath that vampy borrowed dress, I'm willing to bet my entire fortune that your panties are wet.' His eyes glittered. 'The truth is that I'm excited about having sex with you and am counting down the hours until you're honest enough to admit you feel exactly the same way.'

CHAPTER FIVE

THE COCKTAIL PARTY was a crush—a glitzy affair on board an enormous yacht moored in Melbourne's exclusive harbour, filled with socialites and celebrities who had gathered in the city for the big race. The luxury craft bobbed against a backdrop of glittering skyscrapers, an internationally famous rap artist was playing at the far end of the deck and trays of drinks were being circulated by young and very beautiful serving staff who looked like off-duty actors. Very quickly Alejandro was surrounded by a cluster of what looked like adoring fans, leaving Emily standing at the shadowed edge of the exalted golden circle which grew around him.

In truth she'd wanted to skip this party, especially after that disturbing interlude on the sofa. The fact that they'd been so intimate and the fact that she had very nearly succumbed to having sex with him had left her needing to put some very necessary space between her and Alejandro. She didn't think she could bear to keep encountering his mocking green gaze, which was enough to start her heart racing as she remembered his fingers sliding so tantalisingly over her breasts and her thighs.

But it had been about more than the physical. It had been the other stuff, which was way more disturbing. She'd felt connected to him on another level. As if he was the only one who could tap that cold, dark place deep inside her and fill her with warmth and life. Was that being fanciful? Of course it was. She mustn't start inventing fairy tales about him when the reality was apparent, if only she had the courage to face up to it. She was just a frustrated and lonely woman who hadn't been touched like that since she was barely eighteen years old and, in the intervening time, her body must have been simmering away with frustration. It was just a bitter irony that the only man she'd ever cared for was also the man she'd deliberately wounded because she'd been too young and confused to see any other way out.

She had to let it go. She had to or she wouldn't be able to complete the job tasked to her and her professional pride and reputation would be dented. She wanted Alej to see her as someone other than a sexual pushover. Which was why she'd coolly suggested he attend the cocktail party on his own while she tried to claw back some of the hours lost to jet lag. But he had refused point-blank.

'Me stroking your breasts before you deciding you don't want to play along any more doesn't qualify you for dispensation from the job you're being paid to do,' he had drawled. 'You're the official face of my sober new image, Emily, and you're coming to the party with me. You can catch up on your sleep tomorrow, before the race.'

She hated the way he talked about sex so… *casually*…as if it was nothing more than an enjoyable bodily function which could just be enjoyed without much thought or deliberation. Maybe that was how men like him thought of it. When women flung themselves so eagerly at Alej Sabato—herself included—why wouldn't he think of them as anything but sexual fodder? But she had found herself unable to argue with his logic. You couldn't really cite being overly attracted to your boss as a reason for not doing your job properly, could you?

Nonetheless, it had been with a heavy heart that she'd put a few final tweaks to her dishevelled appearance and joined him in the back of the chauffeur-driven car which had brought them down to the harbour. And now she was cast in her favourite role of observer, watching the comings and goings of the glittering guests as she stood in a shadowed corner.

She noticed that, although the party was attended by lots of the hunky drivers who were competing in the race the following day, it was the charismatic Alejandro who captured all the attention. Everyone wanted to talk to him, she realised. She spotted a famous Hollywood actress making her way across the deck to push her way through the small crowd gathered in front of him, her famous fall of blonde hair blowing softly in the early evening breeze. Emily screwed up her nose. Kate Palmer, yes, that was her name—a woman who'd won two BAFTA awards, amongst others. And wasn't that a top-selling novelist surreptitiously sneaking a selfie with him, despite Emily's stern instructions that such casual interactions must stop if he wanted to be taken seriously?

She told herself it was professional pique which was making her so cross that he was ignoring her advice but the truth was a little more sinister. Because a dark rush of jealousy was clenching at her heart, making her want to rush over to the glittering group and to grab

Alej possessively by the arm and to announce that he'd been making love to *her* earlier.

'Must be frustrating.'

A voice made Emily break her gaze from the oddly uncomfortable sight of Alejandro saying something which made the award-winning actress dissolve into instant laughter. Reluctantly she turned her head to study the tanned features of the tall man who had positioned himself beside her, his fair hair and open face making him seem the Argentinian's very antithesis.

'What must?' she asked.

The man shrugged. 'Dating someone like that, who attracts women like moths to the flame. He's famous for it. Or should I say infamous? I saw you come in with him,' he said, by way of an explanation Emily hadn't asked for.

'I'm not dating him,' said Emily slowly.

'No? Well, that's the best news I've heard all evening.' His blue eyes lit up and he extended his hand. 'Marcus Hedlund.'

'Emily Green,' she said as she shook it.

'Happy to meet you, Emily Green. You know, I'm looking for someone who might be interested in sailing away for a year and a day.' He smiled. 'And I've always had a thing about a woman in a red dress. Could I interest you in the position?'

'That's a terribly kind offer,' said Emily sweetly. 'But I'm afraid I'm not in a position to sail anywhere right now—and I'm a terrible sailor anyway.'

'I could teach you. We Swedes make great teachers—didn't you know that?'

Emily smiled back in spite of herself. 'I'm afraid I'm beyond teaching.'

'Nobody is beyond teaching.' Marcus plucked two glasses of champagne from a passing waitress and handed one to Emily and, although she had diligently stuck to fizzy water all evening, she couldn't resist a sip of the fine wine.

'So, back to Sabato,' he continued. 'You're saying he's just…?'

'Just wondering why you're monopolising my newest member of staff,' interjected a voice of steel, and Emily looked up to see that Alejandro had extricated himself from his adoring audience and was standing in front of them, surveying her and Marcus with an unfathomable look darkening his green eyes.

'You were ignoring her, so I stepped in,' said Marcus, giving an unabashed shrug. 'I was simply being chivalrous.'

'Is that what you call it?' queried Alejandro drily. 'Surely you have plenty of women to choose from, Marcus—especially when you own a yacht this size.'

'Not when you're in the vicinity, man. And surely you must know by now that it's not the size of someone's yacht which interests them. Nice to meet you, Emily.' Marcus grinned. 'Don't waste your time falling for him.'

'I don't think there's much chance of that happening,' Emily answered crisply, watching as the Swede raised his glass in a mocking toast and sauntered across the deck, before turning her attention to Alejandro. 'Were you listening to a word I said to you earlier?' she questioned exasperatedly.

He raised his eyebrows. 'Surely I'm the one who should be feeling aggrieved, since I've just found you flirting with one of my oldest friends.'

'I shall flirt with whoever I please. You seem to have no qualms about doing the same. And please don't try to change the subject, Alejandro. I'm serious.'

He could see that. She had assumed a disapproving expression, which seemed at odds with the woman who had briefly come to life like a firecracker in his arms a couple of hours ago.

In her he had seen glimpses of the old Emily, who would thrill to his touch just as he would thrill to hers.

But he hadn't really known her at all back then, had he? He'd attributed to her all kinds of qualities she didn't possess, probably because she'd been an innocent virgin who had made him feel old-fashioned and protective towards her. She had destroyed his idealism with a few cruel words and, because of his dalliance with her, his mother had been summarily dismissed from her job.

He felt a beat of anger as he remembered his impotent rage when he'd heard about his mother's sacking, but anger was a pointless emotion. Desire was something he was better equipped to deal with. And revenge, of course. A primitive reaction but a very satisfying one, nonetheless. He hid his flicker of anticipation behind a bland mask of social concern.

'Would you like some food?' he questioned.

'No, thanks. I'm allergic to caviar. I'm going to head back to the hotel and do a little work before getting an early night.'

'I'll come with you.'

'No, Alejandro,' she said, in a low voice. 'You stay on here. People will be disappointed if you leave now. You're obviously the guest of honour and you don't need me hanging around. Besides, that actress you were talking to has been staring at you with moony eyes for the last five minutes.'

His eyes narrowed. 'I thought you told me women were off limits?'

'Women in the *plural*, not the singular! If you…' She drew in a deep breath and seemed to be having difficulty finding the right words. 'If you've decided you want to enter into a normal relationship with someone, that would be…fine. In fact, it would be more than fine and I can't see that having an actress as a consort would act as a deterrent to your political ambition. It's hardly mould-breaking, is it?'

'So you're giving me your consent to date her?'

Her mouth flattened. 'You don't need my consent to date anyone. You're as much of a free agent as I am. Just try not to make too much noise if you decide to bring her back to the suite tonight, will you? I'll take your car to the hotel and send the driver straight back. Goodnight.'

With that, she was gone, giving him a brief smile as she turned to leave, and Alej was left feeling distinctly outmanoeuvred as he stared at her retreating form. Shiny strands of dark blonde hair were dangling at the back of her neck and her skirt was a scarlet sheen as it swished enticingly against her bottom.

The actress was heading towards him but he barely noticed her—he was too outraged by Emily's liberal attitude as a myriad previously unknown and buttoned-up prejudices came flooding to the forefront of his mind. Was she really giving him the thumbs-up to bring another woman to his bed tonight, when he had been doing some fairly intimate things to *her* a few hours earlier? Especially when she was sleeping just a few yards down the corridor? His mouth hardened with disapproval. Was that the type of free-love world she operated in these days?

'Alej?'

It was the classically trained voice of Kate Palmer, her short Grecian-style dress showing a lot of honed and gleaming thigh. Slanting him a slow smile, she ran her fingers through her defining fall of hair with the deliberate nonchalance of someone who spent much of her life being watched.

'I wondered where you were.'

'Standing right here,' he said. 'As you see.'

'Do you fancy going on somewhere else?' she questioned, just a fraction too casually.

'I've been invited to a party in Kooyong and we were all thinking of going on to the casino later. Should be a good crowd.'

Alej studied her. She had the twin cachet of beauty and fame and most men wouldn't have thought twice about accepting an offer he suspected she didn't have to make very often. His indifference towards her wasn't feigned and yet it infuriated him that all he could think about was Emily and the insouciant way she'd left him standing there. Was she playing games with him, he wondered—or did she still get off with the kind of foreplay which threatened to drive a man insane?

He realised that the actress was still looking at him with confident expectation and curved his mouth into a regretful smile—because who was to say he mightn't take her up on her offer sometime in the future?

'Not tonight, I'm afraid. Early night for me,' he explained. 'It's the big race tomorrow.'

She quickly recovered her obvious disappointment and slanted him another smile. 'Of course. Good luck. Isn't one of your drivers in pole position?'

His heart wasn't in it but he forced himself to continue the predictable conversation about his team's chances, giving her time to

beat a dignified retreat before he left the bob-
bing yacht and went in search of his car. The
city was alive with a pre-race buzz of excitement and people were spilling out of bars and
restaurants, but all Alej was aware of during
the journey back to the hotel was the insidi-
ous invasion of desire. It heated his blood and
licked at his skin. It was making him distinctly
uncomfortable as his trousers strained over the
throbbing hardness at his groin. His mouth was
dry and his heart was racing as he entered the
hotel and when the elevator deposited him in
the penthouse suite, he found himself hoping
against hope that Emily hadn't gone to bed.

She hadn't.

She was lying on the black leather sofa and
she was fast asleep. His heart missed a beat.
She'd changed from the borrowed red party
frock and slipped into a pair of wide yoga
pants and a sleeveless vest, against which her
breasts rose and fell in time with her steady
breathing. Before her a half-drunk cup of herb
tea stood next to her computer and the closely
written notebook she'd been referring to earlier. She'd let down her hair, so that it surrounded her head like a flaxen pillow, and it
was that more than anything which had Alej
transfixed as he stood in the doorway, feeling

like a voyeur, not just to her, but to the past they had once shared.

Because she used to wear her hair flowing down her back like that when she'd been seventeen, when he used to run his fingers wonderingly through the lustrous thickness, as if it were pure, spun gold, blending into the pillow they'd made of the hay bale. He thought about just going to bed and leaving her there—except that she'd wake up cold and uncomfortable and she wouldn't be able to work unless she was properly rested. At least, that was what he convinced himself was his motive as he began to move towards her. As he glanced down at the table he could see she'd been drawing grids and a big triangle, around which different letters were scattered so that it looked like one of those mathematical equations he'd thankfully been spared due to his lack of schooling. Right in the centre of the page the letter M was written, with a big red circle around it and a series of question marks beside it.

'Emily?' he said softly.

'Alej!' Her eyelashes fluttered open and she stirred, rubbing her fist over her eyes. 'Sorry. I must have fallen asleep. Obviously.' She yawned. 'What time is it?'

She flicked him a heavy-lidded gaze and

once again he felt his heart contract, because hadn't she looked at him like that plenty of times before, in that sleepy, trusting way? Those times when she'd made him feel he could conquer the world. That everything she needed, he could provide for her. But his body had been the only thing she'd wanted, he reminded himself savagely. And maybe it still was.

'It's still early,' he said evenly.

'Oh.' She struggled up into a sitting position. 'Is the party over?'

But Alej didn't want to make polite small talk. He didn't want to pretend he felt nothing as he looked down at her blonde and ruffled beauty. 'Were those other men you left me for as good as me, Emily?' he questioned suddenly.

'I'm sorry?'

'You heard me.'

She blinked at him and he could see a faint colour begin to wash over her pale cheeks. 'What on earth has brought all this on?'

'Seriously. I want to know. Were they as big as me? Did they make you come as easily as I did?'

She was frowning now, half in confusion and half with something else. Something which made her tongue slide out of her mouth to moisten her lips. 'Alej. Are you out of your mind? What on earth has brought all this on? Stop it,' she whispered.

'But you don't want me to stop it, Emily. You never did. That much hasn't changed.'

His green eyes were burning into her, making her skin feel as if it were on fire, and Emily knew she should get straight off that sofa and head for the sanctuary of her bedroom. But somehow she couldn't seem to bring herself to move—because the trouble was that he was right. She *didn't* want him to stop—she wanted him to carry on talking dirty to her all night long and looking at her in that hungry way, as if he wanted to ravish her. The blunt sexual boasts were turning her on, as she guessed they were supposed to, and the warning narrative spinning around her head wasn't strong enough to withstand the increasingly urgent demands of her body.

And suddenly Emily had no real desire to fight them. Why would she when she'd been living without physical contact for so long? When most times she felt more like a piece of stone rather than a flesh-and-blood woman. Had abstinence brought her any pleasure or felt even a little bit worthwhile? No way. It had served only to make her isolated—but then, she'd always felt like that. She'd always been the person on the outside who was looking in. The daughter who was nothing but a burden to a socially ambitious mother and then the stepdaughter who had got in the way. Alej had been the only person who had ever made her feel as if she mattered.

He was smiling now. That slow killer smile which always used to get her. She hadn't been able to resist it then and it seemed she couldn't resist it now.

Feeling like someone caught up in a dark spell, Emily obeyed the Argentinian's wordless command, and opened her arms to him.

CHAPTER SIX

'*GUAU!*' THE WORD escaped from Alej's lips like a murmured curse as he sank on top of Emily's soft and eager body and felt the first contact of her breasts. He could feel the hard thrust of her nipples pinpointing into his chest as he pulled her closer, his hands sliding down to reacquaint themselves with her legs. Blood pooled into his groin as he stroked her thighs through the soft cotton of her yoga pants.

'Alej,' she moaned as if she was asking him a question, but he didn't press her to elaborate because it was pretty obvious what she wanted—judging from the urgent way she was circling her hips against the rocky pole of his erection like some kind of wildcat on heat.

Once again the thought of another man doing this to her filled him with a blind rage but, ruthlessly, he drove it from his mind. Because anger and jealousy would detract from his purpose and all he needed to think about was this one thing. Of losing himself deep inside her and riding her to fulfilment. Ridding himself of this damned fever which had lain dormant inside him for too long and been brought to a head when he'd seen her standing with the Argentinian sun bouncing off her blonde hair and her arms around a mangy horse's neck.

He'd thought that time might have diluted his reaction to her and when he saw her again he would feel nothing but indifference. But he had been wrong. Badly wrong. Because every night since that recent meeting he had dreamt of her. Had imagined doing this to her. Touching every inch of her curvy frame and then plunging into her tight wetness—long and hard and deep. He wanted sex and nothing more, but first he needed to assess whether she wanted the same.

'*Que quieres?*' he demanded roughly.

She shook the head which was slumped against his shoulder, as if words were beyond her, but Alej asked again. He needed to ask it, even if the idea of her refusal was unendurable. But he would endure it. Hadn't he endured more than most men would have to face in a lifetime? Reaching to turn her face towards his, her shuddered breath warm against his fingers, he asked again, this time in English. 'What do you want, Emily?'

'You!' she burst out, as if an inner floodgate had opened inside her. 'I want you!'

It felt like a triumph, but only a momentary one because the exquisite ache between his legs was warning Alej that he needed to keep his wits about him or this would be over too quickly. Already he wanted to explode like a teenage boy on his first time and that wasn't going to happen, for he had waited too long to squander a single second of this.

His mouth found her neck, the tip of his tongue trailing a feather-light path along its surface, which quickly had her wriggling with pleasure. His groin bucked as she circled her hips against him with urgent hunger, which made his heart race. He had forgotten just how responsive she was. How her receptive body thrilled to just about anything he did to her. Maybe that was because the two of them had taken foreplay to a whole new level and then redefined it. There had been long months of denying themselves that final penetration and when they had...

Against her neck, his lips hardened.

When they had...

Bitterness rushed through him but he forced himself to shelve it because nothing was going to detract from this. He could feel her moving against him, turning her head towards his face in silent plea. She wanted him to kiss her, he knew that. But he didn't want to kiss her—at least, not there. He didn't want to do anything which might masquerade as true affection and he certainly wasn't going to give her the pleasure of imagining he felt anything for her other than lust. Because he didn't. The only thing he wanted from Emily Green was her body. Her sweet and tempting body.

With a low growl he got off the sofa and then bent down to pick her up in his arms. She was heavier than she looked but he liked that. He liked the solidity of her firm flesh as he carried her through the enormous room, past the white piano and colourful displays of flowers. Past the giant picture windows with their views over the Melbourne rooftops and the skyscrapers which were glittering like jewels in the night.

'Where…where are we going?' she gasped.

'Where do you think we're going? To discuss some of your "clear objectives"?' he growled sarcastically. 'I'm taking you to bed.'

Her eyes were huge and dark as she stared

up at him. 'We've never…we've never actually been to bed before,' she whispered.

It was both the right thing and the wrong thing to say. It filled him first with fury and then with intent. Because he had only ever been good enough for the stable, hadn't he? Hidden away like some guilty secret amid the spiky bales of straw. Played with as if he were a puppet. She'd had him on the end of a string and whenever she had tugged it, he'd come running, hadn't he? The low-born illegitimate son of a servant who had been punching well above his weight by romancing the rich man's stepdaughter. Well, the tables had most definitely turned, he thought grimly, as he planted his foot in the centre of the door and shoved it open with a forceful kick.

'No, we haven't. And right here just happens to be about the biggest and most luxurious bed you can imagine,' he said as the door swung shut silently behind them and he carried her towards the snowy-covered king-size. 'Don't they say the best things in life are worth waiting for?'

A trickle of apprehension ran down Emily's spine as Alejandro's words washed over her like dark silk and she wondered if it was just her imagination or whether they were under-

pinned with danger. For one terrifying moment
of clarity she wondered how she had allowed
this situation to arise—just as she wondered if
there was still a chance to come to her senses
and put a stop to it. But the truth was that she
didn't want to, even if such a thing were possible. Because by then he had laid her down
on top of the bedcover and was peeling off her
vest top and the last of her misgivings were
dissolved by the sweet touch of his fingers
against her bare skin.

The sexual hunger which he had ignited earlier now began to build to an unbearable pitch
as he touched her. Like somebody with a bad
fever, she was trembling uncontrollably as he
began to explore her skin, murmuring something in Spanish which she'd never heard him
say before. Was she imagining that it sounded
almost like *anger*? But by then he was sliding
down her yoga pants so she was lying there
in just her bra and knickers. Almost thought-
fully he ran his finger around the dip of her
navel, circling it ever so slowly before moving it down towards her sensible cotton pants.
To make it easy for him, Emily parted her
thighs and felt herself stiffen with growing
excitement.

'Oh,' she said.

'Oh, what?' he mimicked lazily as he whispered his fingertip lightly over the already damp gusset.

Her heart started punching loudly in her chest and she felt almost bashful as hot colour flooded her cheeks. But this wasn't the time or the place for shyness, she told herself. It wasn't as if they'd never done this before. But the weird thing was that, although she'd been more intimate with him than with any other man, the fact remained that right now he seemed like a very sexy stranger and it was making her a little bit apprehensive.

Stop thinking like that, she urged herself. Concentrate on the pleasure he's giving you. 'That feels so good,' she managed, because surely that was the sort of thing she should be saying.

'Does it?' She could hear the smile in his voice. 'I haven't even started yet, Emily.'

'I'd forgotten…'

'What?' he prompted softly, his finger still teasing her with those unbearable feather-light little touches.

As her eyelids fluttered helplessly to a close, Emily thought about telling him the unvarnished truth. She'd forgotten how he could make every inch of her body feel like a newly discovered erogenous zone. She'd forgotten because she'd made herself forget—along with all the other X-rated memories of the things they'd done together. Like the time he'd once made her come with his fingertip stroking the crotch of her jeans, instantly arousing her despite the barrier of the thick denim—and she had felt so deliciously grown-up and decadent as she'd stood shuddering in a darkened corner of the stable. She'd filed away those recollections because they seemed to have belonged to another time and another person. They certainly bore no resemblance to the sexually barren woman she had become.

'I don't remember,' she breathed.

'What a pity,' he mocked. 'I was waiting with bated breath.'

He stopped touching her and stepped away from the bed to begin removing his own clothes and, although Emily was aware that she was behaving passively, somehow she felt powerless to respond in any other way. Because wasn't she afraid he'd discover that he was the only man she'd ever had sex with? Wouldn't that slightly laughable admission display her vulnerability and leave her open to being hurt? Wouldn't it be like handing him a great big fistful of power, when he already had much more than her? So she said nothing and lay back on the bedcovers, watching him. And, oh, he was definitely worth watching.

She'd only ever seen him removing casual and dusty clothes, either jodhpurs or jeans, not an immaculate lightweight suit which must have cost a small fortune. But the end result was the same—it didn't matter if he wore denim or silk, it was the body beneath which was the ultimate jewel. Shrugging off his jacket, he unbuttoned his silk shirt to reveal his honed and gleaming chest, and Emily's heart pounded with delighted recognition as she ran her gaze hungrily over it.

Could any man be as beautiful as Alejandro Sabato? she wondered longingly. His limbs were long and strong and his washboard abs reminded her of the disciplined way he'd always lived. The way he'd exercised his hard body until it was coated with sweat. Her gaze moved further down as he unzipped his suit trousers, letting them fall to the ground before kicking off his suede moccasins, so that he was left standing in nothing but a pair of dark and silky boxer shorts. And how could she look anywhere other than at the tantalising line of dark hair which ran downwards, drawing her attention to the rocky bulge at his crotch?

Did he see where she was looking? Was that why he stroked his fingertips over the steely outline of his erection with deliberate provocation, so that she bit her lip with frustrated voyeurism as colour flooded into her cheeks?

'Frustrated, Emily?' he questioned softly, but there was a definite touch of cruelty and control edging his question.

A number of answers sprang to Emily's mind, though it was difficult to concentrate on anything when she was being confronted by such a glorious sight. She could have asked him not to tease her. Not to use his expertise and mastery to make her feel even more inexperienced than she was. But she needed to grab back some control. She was no longer a nearly eighteen-year-old virgin whose whole world revolved around a dashing young polo player she'd known since she was twelve, but a woman of twenty-six. If she was going to have sex with Alejandro—which she certainly was, or else she wouldn't have been lying here naked and aching while watching him undress—then shouldn't it be on as level a playing field as possible?

So she levered herself up onto her elbows, noticing the way his gaze swivelled to the bounce of her breasts as she did so, before fixing him with a steady look. She thought about all those films she'd seen—where confident women smiled, as if it was perfectly normal to have sex and to say exactly what it was you were feeling inside. Or not feeling. Concentrate on the sensation, she told herself—and leave emotion out of it.

'Yes, I'm a little bit frustrated. Surely you must be, too,' she answered, with the flicker of a smile as she removed her bra and pants with hands which weren't as still as she would have liked them to be. 'So why don't you hurry up and get over here?'

That shocked him. Of course it did. She suspected he was a little bit old-fashioned at heart and she would never have said anything like that before—not in a million years. She watched his face momentarily darken before he dropped his shorts, walking towards her with supreme confidence in his aroused nakedness, in a way she doubted any other man could match.

'You mean like this?' he questioned as he lowered himself down on her.

'Yes,' she breathed. 'I mean exactly like that.'

'Are you going to tell me how best you like it?'

'I'll…' The word came out in a gasp. 'I'll leave that to you.'

Alej positioned himself so that his weight was on his elbows, putting him in a perfect position to see the darkness of her sapphire eyes. Her lips were parting and their moist gleam was enticing but still he couldn't bring himself to kiss her. So instead he ran the tip of his tongue down her neck and then to her chest, before making a moist path along the hollow between her breasts. He could taste the salt of her sweat and she moaned a little as he moved his head to concentrate on one pert mound, teasing the nipple until it was rose-dark and puckered before turning his attention to the other breast.

'That's…'

'What?' he prompted huskily as the word was bitten off by her teeth digging into her bottom lip.

'Amazing,' she breathed.

'I should hope so.' He smiled before sliding his tongue over her belly and as he sensed her growing frustration, that somehow pleased him. Restlessly, she tried to lift her hips in impatient demand but he stilled her by teasing light circles over her skin before tiptoeing his fingers down towards the soft bush at her groin. Her little moans had stopped and he could tell she was holding her breath, wanting him to touch her where she most wanted to be touched. For a while he teased her some more by holding off and when his middle finger alighted on her sweet spot and began to strum, she almost shot off the bed, convulsively clutching him by the shoulders. And as her nails dug into his flesh, Alej felt a brief flare of something he couldn't define. Maybe it was his own little bit of rebellion which made him wonder how she would deal with it if he calmly removed himself from her body and told her he'd changed his mind.

But he couldn't. Even though she had betrayed him and treated him like dirt. Even though hers had been the first act in a chain of events which was to darken his life for ever, he couldn't pull back. Even if he were about to die, he couldn't think of anywhere else he'd rather be right now, with the warm, potent scent of sex in the air, and the only sound their shuddered breathing as he felt himself grow so hard that he wanted to explode. He'd planned to make her come every which way— first with his finger and then with his mouth. He'd planned to further increase his desire by making himself wait before finally thrusting into her molten heat and driving up to the very hilt of her, but he could see now that wasn't going to be a possibility. He wanted her now.

'Oh!'

She made a single syllable of disappointment as he withdrew his finger from her sticky heat.

'Always so impatient,' he observed.

Her teeth were digging into her lower lip again and now there was anxious query in her sapphire eyes, as if she'd suddenly realised he'd been having second thoughts. 'Alej?'

He paused for just long enough to make her anxiety real before he relented. 'Don't worry, *querida*,' he whispered. 'I'll be right back. But first I need to get some protection.'

She nodded. 'Of course.'

As he removed himself from the bed, Emily was overcome with a rush of remorse and shame. What was the matter with her? Was Alej aware that if he hadn't intervened she would have happily taken him unprotected into her body, desperate to feel his unsheathed hardness inside her? How insane would that have been—if she'd ended up pregnant with Alej's child? Yet the idea didn't fill her with the horror it surely should have done. Instead she got a frighteningly vivid image of herself cradling a black-haired baby in her arms and she experienced a pang of something which felt like wistfulness. Or regret.

It was only when he turned his back on her to dig into the pocket of his suit trousers that she noticed the scar which snaked across his back—a livid zigzag, dark red and angry against the olive skin. It was the only disfigurement on an otherwise perfect physique but it was big enough to make her gasp out loud.

He must have heard her because he turned around—the glint of the foil condom matching the sudden forbidding glint of his eyes.

'Oh, Alej. Whatever happened to your back?' she whispered.

'I don't want to talk about it. Especially not right now.'

'But it's—'

'I *said*, I don't want to talk about it. Do you want me to repeat it in Spanish?'

The harsh note of finality in his voice was deterrent enough, but by then he was back beside her and suddenly the scar was forgotten. Everything was forgotten and her attention was inevitably drawn to other things as he opened the foil with exaggerated care before stroking it onto the erection which was nudging hard against his belly. A wave of something like shyness washed over her as she saw how aroused he was and Emily's heart warred with her mind about what it was she was expecting from this. Her body had certainly been brought to life and already she felt poised on an erotic knife-edge, where the slightest thing would send her hurtling over the edge. But something was missing. Something she couldn't put her finger on.

'Now,' murmured Alejandro as he moved over her and she could feel his hardness pressing against her. 'Where were we?'

She was running her fingertips hungrily over his bare back, her fingertips encountering the raised surface of the zigzagging scar for the first time. But he shifted his position slightly and she said nothing more about the disfigurement, concentrating instead on his husky question. 'I'm not…sure,' she answered.

'Then how about I remind you, Princesa?'

It was a long time since he'd called her that but this time the nickname was underpinned with a harshness which had never been there before, which in any other circumstance might have made Emily think twice about what was about to happen. But it was already too late. He was licking her breasts and her blood was pulsing warm and thick as she felt the experienced flick of his fingers against her clitoris. She heard him murmur his approval and then her thighs were spreading open as if no power in the world could stop them and he was entering her. He was pushing deep inside the slickness which awaited him and filling her completely. Emily moaned and instantly he stilled, his eyes narrowed in question.

'It's good?'

Wordlessly, she nodded. Of course it was. It was better than good. Better than anything she'd ever experienced—but it was a shock, too. Alejandro had always been big—not that she had anyone to compare him to, of course— but their first time together had been so loaded with emotion that she hadn't had time to appreciate it properly in the way she could now. But she couldn't tell him that. She didn't want to stir up bad feelings about the past and neither did she want to confess to another possibility—that her body had become unaccommodating and tight in all the intervening years, because it had been so starved of pleasure.

So she put her hands on his shoulders and sucked in a deep breath. 'Is it good for you, too?'

'Oh, Emily. You have no idea,' he groaned in response. 'Especially when you play the part of breathless little innocent so effectively. Aren't you a little old to be cast in the role of disingenuous virgin?'

For a moment she scented more danger. He thought she was playing games, or acting a part? That this was just a cynical approach she was adopting to inject a little excitement into their lovemaking? She wanted to tell him the truth—that this was so beautiful that deep down she *did* feel as innocent as the first time she'd lain with him. But she guessed he would dismiss such an idealistic sentiment and, anyway, her thoughts were blotted out by his next potent thrust.

At first his movements were slow—as if he was determined to emphasise how utterly he filled her—and Emily was taken aback by how intimate it felt. One flesh, she found herself thinking. Was that why those stupid tears began to prick at the backs of her eyes, forcing her to blink them away before he saw them? Why she turned her face to search for his kiss, only to realise that he was far more intent on bending his dark head to lick at her nipple? But then his movements grew more rapid as he shafted up deep inside her and all her doubts were put on the back burner because suddenly Emily was rediscovering sex—big time. His body was hard and powerful. His skin felt like satin against her fingers and she was like a woman possessed as she writhed beneath him, moaning things like, 'Please…' and, 'Oh, yes…' and, 'Yes, that… *That.*'

'You mean like that?' he clarified, with-drawing almost completely before driving up deep inside her again.

'Yes…yes…' she breathed. 'Exactly like that.'

And then it happened, almost without her expecting it—that heady rush of promise which morphed into perfect bliss as her world exploded into countless dazzling stars. Emily clung to him, crying out helplessly as her body spasmed around him before she heard his own shuddered moan and felt his driving jerks as he spilled his seed inside her. Spent, he collapsed on top of her and those next few moments were the closest thing to sanctuary she'd felt in a long time. For a while she just lay there, co-cooned in his strong arms, feeling as if she were floating on some warm and rippling sea until Alejandro's words shot into her thoughts and scattered them like a spray gun.

'I certainly wasn't expecting it to be quite so easy,' he remarked.

'Easy?' she echoed, wondering if she might have misheard him.

'Mmm…' He turned onto his side and stared at her, his green gaze smoky and assessing. 'But I'd forgotten how hot you were. Hotter than any other woman I've ever had.'

Emily didn't answer straight away. You don't have to answer, she told herself. You're not on some game show with the clock ticking away. You can take as much time as you want. All the time you need to get your head around the fact that you have just *slept with your boss.*

Unwrapping his arm from where it was coiled so comfortably around her waist, Emily rolled away from him. It would be tempting to jump up from the bed. To grab her clothes and rush from the room—maybe even slamming the door behind her so that it echoed through the vast penthouse suite. But that wouldn't be the behaviour of someone who was mature and responsible, would it? It was difficult to come back from something as dramatic as that, and didn't they need to move on—or not—from what had just happened? He thought she was easy—and could she really blame him? So why not go along with that? Let him think she was sexually rapacious, just as he was. Especially since the alternative was to wail and wonder why she'd done such a stupid thing, which ran the risk of making her look both reckless and indiscriminate.

So she fanned her face exaggeratedly with her hand. 'Thanks.'

He looked momentarily perplexed. 'Thanks?'

'Mmm… It's always nice to be described as hot,' she remarked blandly, seeing his face inexplicably darken in response. 'Quite literally in this case. Boiling hot, actually—despite the air conditioning. Any chance you could rustle us up a glass of water, Alej?'

He looked outraged—there was no other word for it—but Emily told herself she didn't care. What good would it do her if she fell back into his arms and told him that she was only ever hot with him? Such an admission would show weakness and she'd already made herself weak enough in his eyes.

But despite his obvious disapproval of her question, he nonetheless accommodated her wishes, sauntering out of the bedroom in all his glorious nakedness and giving her time to snap the light on and scramble back into her clothes. He seemed unsurprised to find her fully dressed when he returned minutes later with the requested water and—rather disturbingly—the notebook she'd been scribbling in earlier, just before her jet-lagged state had caused her to pass out on the sofa. He yawned and positioned himself back on the bed, waiting until she had gulped down half a glass of water before holding the notebook aloft.

'What's this?' he questioned, his finger jabbing at the grid diagrams she had drawn earlier.

She shrugged. 'It's life-coach stuff I use when I'm working with new clients. You know. All about reality and perception and fixed ideas. I'm guessing you probably don't want a complete breakdown of the meanings?'

'You're right. I don't.'

'Mainly it's about what it is possible to change in your life,' she elaborated, as still he continued to look at her enquiringly.

'And the *M*?'

There was a pause as Emily felt her cheeks growing warm. 'You're contemplating a massive change and you probably need to simplify your life. Stop jet-setting quite so much and make more of a base in Argentina, especially as that's going to be your home when you go into politics.'

'I asked about the *M*,' he emphasised silkily. 'Which you have circled and underlined several times.'

The hotness in her cheeks increased. 'Part of your "problem"—which plenty of men wouldn't actually define as a problem—'

'Get to the point, Emily.'

She drew in a deep breath and watched his gaze flicker to the wobble of her breasts. 'Is the woman thing.'

'The woman thing?'

She nodded. 'That's what lets you down every time. Not just the book Colette wrote, which was probably motivated by bitterness that you didn't marry her. But also the way you seem to attract women like a magnet. Like Marcus said earlier—you can't seem to help it. The online edition of one of the Australian tabloids is even carrying a photo of you taken with Kate Palmer tonight—there must have been a long-lens photographer at the harbour. And the author who took a surreptitious selfie at the same party has already put it up on her social-media page—and she's got over thirty-one thousand followers.'

'None of this is new,' he pointed out.

'No, but it only fuels your reputation as a commitment-phobe who plays the field like mad—and those are not the kind of qualities which ordinary people want from the person who is representing them.' Somehow she met his bright green gaze without flinching. 'The *M* stands for marriage. You need a wife, Alej. And before you look at me that way, why not? Would-be politicians have been making judicious marriages since the beginning of time. It would be an instant badge of commitment and respectability which would only help your career.'

'But I don't want to get married,' he observed caustically. 'I never did. Not with Colette. Not with anyone.'

She shrugged. 'And that's your dilemma.'

Yes.

His dilemma.

Or maybe not.

From his vantage point on top of the rumpled bedclothes, Alej studied the woman with whom he'd just had the best sex he could remember, and yet here she was calmly discussing his marriage to someone else. A wave of something like bitterness ran through him. Was she really such a hard-hearted bitch that she could coolly advocate he go and find himself a wife and not really *care*? Did he mean so little to her? *Of course he did. Nothing new there, either.* Yet the irony of the situation didn't escape him because deep down he knew that if she'd displayed sadness and resentment at the thought of him marrying someone else, she wouldn't have seen him for dust.

But maybe *Emily* was exactly what he needed. For now, at least. He'd thought she'd cared for him all those years ago but he'd been wrong, just as he'd been wrong about so many things. But back then she had been barely eighteen with the world at her feet. She must have believed anything was possible and had since discovered that it was not. Because surely it hadn't been her life's ambition to end up running some crummy little business and living in a tiny London apartment. Didn't she miss the riches she had grown up with while she lived in Argentina and the kind of lifestyle which came as part of the whole package?

Even more pertinently, wouldn't she have learnt by now that no other man came close to him when it came to giving her physical pleasure? Her gushing and instant response whenever he touched her would seem to indicate so. Wouldn't marriage add a deliciously dark element to the revenge he was determined to extract from her? Wouldn't it ensure she would never really forget him, because what woman ever forgot the man who slid a golden ring onto her finger?

'I think you could be right, Emily,' he said, easing himself up on the bank of squashed pillows and slanting her a slow smile. 'I need a temporary bride—and you are the obvious candidate.'

CHAPTER SEVEN

THERE WAS A moment of stillness, when time seemed to be suspended as Emily stared at Alej in astonishment. Her nails dug into the bed sheet. He had just asked her to marry him! The hunky Argentinian billionaire had just asked her to be his bride! And wasn't it weird how easily the mind could distort reality and allow fantasy to take over for a few disbelieving seconds? Why else would a rush of joy have flooded through her body at the thought of being joined with the man she had once loved so fiercely? The man who could still make her feel more alive than anyone else. Who, even now, could take her into his arms and make her dissolve with longing.

Until she reminded herself that this was no romantic moonlit proposal, inspired by his certainty that they were meant for each other and he couldn't live without her. This was a cold and calculated public-relations exercise. A marriage made not in heaven, but within the scribbled pages of a moleskin notebook—by her!

She prayed that she'd managed to hide her initial delight because if Alej had any idea how much the idea had thrilled her, it would put her in a poor bargaining position. But she didn't have to bargain with him, she reminded herself. She was a free agent. An employee. And yes, she'd just had sex with him, but so what? She certainly didn't have to marry him.

'Is that a joke?' she questioned as coolly as she could, though her heart was still crashing against her ribcage and she found herself wondering if he'd be able to notice its thundering movement beneath her vest.

'You know it isn't.'

She stared up at him—sprawled there unashamedly, his naked olive body outlined against the white covers. His eyes were bright, his jaw much darker than usual, and he exuded the air of a man who was physically satisfied. He looked utterly delectable and completely sexy—but she wasn't going to think about that. She couldn't afford to. 'You must realise that I can't possibly marry you, Alej.'

'Why not?' he said.

'Because…because it's a crazy idea.' She

shook her head, trying to inject some conviction into her voice as she found herself fantasising about a big white dress and a bunch of scented flowers the size of a rugby ball. What was the *matter* with her? She got up off the bed, mainly to protect herself from the allure of his proximity. 'Crazy,' she repeated.

Outside, the moon was gleaming silver over the Melbourne skyscrapers and the sense that she was living in some strange kind of parallel universe descended on her again. As if she would ever take part in a marriage of convenience to a man she'd once been in love with! Wouldn't that be like playing a kind of high-stakes emotional Russian roulette, with her the guaranteed loser?

She drank some more water and then walked over to the window, still trying to get her head around what had happened. The sex had been amazing, but something had been missing during that erotic encounter which had definitely been there before. Something in him. It had taken a while for her to work out what it was, and the answer had arrived in a heart-sinking moment of understanding. Because he hadn't been like the loving and tender Alej of old. He had been like a machine, not a man. A warm, breathing machine who could bestow inordinate amounts of pleasure—but a machine nonetheless.

And she was most definitely not a machine. She had never felt so vibrantly and deliciously *alive* and the reason for that was because Alej had awoken something in her. Something which thrilled her because she'd thought she'd lost it for ever—the ability to feel emotional intensity and physical pleasure. But her reaction scared her, too. Because wasn't it dangerous to feel those things, when the man involved had a heart of ice?

'Before you give me all the reasons why you shouldn't,' he said, 'let me list some of the reasons why you should.'

She sank down into a cross-legged position on a white leather window seat and stared at him. 'Go ahead.'

'I will pay you a lot of money to be my wife,' he said tonelessly. 'For a limited period, of course.'

'Of course you will, Alej. You're a very rich man.'

She could see in his green eyes a flicker of scorn, and his lips twisted as he spoke.

'Don't tell me the thought of a seven-figure sum doesn't turn you on, Emily?'

It was a vulgar statement, which made her

wonder what kind of circles he'd been mixing in. The same kind as her mother, probably, she reflected painfully. The ones where women made no secret of adoring diamonds and fast cars and luxury yachts anchored in city harbours. *Did he think she was cut from the same cloth as the woman who had birthed her?* 'Money often creates more problems than it solves,' she suggested.

'An admirable sentiment. Though one I find difficult to believe and only ever expressed by people who don't have any.' He paused, his green eyes glinting. 'If the money offends you, then give it to charity—nobody is stopping you from being altruistic. Think about it, Emily,' he urged silkily.

So she did. She thought about being able to help Great-Aunt Jane. To *really* help the woman who had sacrificed so much for Emily's mother and been given barely a word of thanks in return. The last time her mother had entered rehab to try to conquer her tranquilliser addiction, it had been Emily's great-aunt who had somehow managed to scrabble together enough money to pick up the bill. At the time it had been doable—just—because Jane had been working as a legal secretary, but now she was existing on a tiny pension and getting frailer by the day. Wouldn't it be *great* to free her from the worry of future medical bills incurred by the inevitability of aging? To not just present her with a one-off cheque, but enough money to look after her for the rest of her days.

Emily bit her lip as she thought about being able to take a proper holiday herself—her first in years, because she'd been ploughing all her time and any spare money into the business. She could wear a floppy hat and sarong and finally get to read the stack of books stashed away by her bed back home. There would probably even be enough to pay off some of her mortgage. Wouldn't it be good to cut herself a bit of slack for once?

But none of these considerations addressed the way she felt about Alej, because she recognised that marriage would be a velvet-lined trap, which would pose all kinds of hidden dangers. She'd just had sex with him and she couldn't seem to control her reaction whenever he laid a finger on her. So what if her feelings for him intensified? What if she found herself falling in love with him all over again? She couldn't do it. For sanity's sake, she must refuse.

'No, Alej.'

He gave a slow smile. 'Before you give me

your final answer, perhaps it is time for me to be blunt—as you English sometimes say.'

'That remark is usually the forerunner to some kind of insult.'

'Or a home truth, perhaps?' He ran a lazy finger reflectively along the sensual outline of his lips. 'You are—how old, now?'

She wanted to tell him that he knew exactly how old she was, but maybe he didn't. Maybe she was crediting herself with more importance in his memory than she really had and he'd simply forgotten. 'Twenty-six.' His eyes were boring into her. Was it that which made her elaborate, like a child trying to make themselves seem more mature? 'Nearly twenty-seven, actually.'

He nodded. 'And there has been no engagement? No close brushes with marriage?'

Her heart squeezed because his interrogation felt painful for all kinds of reasons. It made her feel like a failure and it made her feel like a bit of a freak. 'No.'

'Ever lived with anyone?'

'No again.'

'In that case, I will be doing you an enormous favour, Emily.'

She screwed up her face in genuine confusion. 'How do you work that one out?'

Did she imagine the flicker of pleasure which lifted the corners of his lips and the glint of triumph which sparked in the depths of his green eyes?

'A man who has never married is seen as something of a catch. As sexy and elusive,' he murmured. 'Unfortunately, it is not the same for a woman since she loses her appeal with each year that passes.'

It was a good thing she wasn't still holding her glass of water because Emily honestly thought she might have hurled it at his patronising head. But at least his outrageous comment propelled her out of the numbness caused by his shock proposal of marriage. 'Did you decide to throw all the feminist textbooks onto a bonfire of your own arrogance?' she hissed at him, the serenity of her yoga pose forgotten. 'Or are you just going out of your way to insult me—as I suspected from the beginning?'

'Please don't shoot the messenger. I am merely telling it how it is,' he said calmly, with an expansive shrug of his broad, bare shoulders. He pillowed his ruffled black head back against crossed arms and studied her reflectively. 'But if you were a divorcee,' he mused, 'and a rich one, to boot…that would immediately make you attractive to all kinds of men.

Which means you'd have a lot more chance of finding yourself a suitable partner in the future.'

Even though she knew her reaction was deeply irrational, Emily found herself hurt by the things he was saying. But why shouldn't he talk about her long-term future so objectively and with no role for him to play in it, when that was the reality? Yes, he'd had sex with her and, yes, he was offering her a bizarre kind of marriage—but he wasn't doing it because he had *feelings* for her. And although she could see the undoubted benefits of him taking a temporary bride—hadn't she suggested it herself?—she sensed he wasn't telling her the whole story.

'I'm getting a strong suspicion that your desire to bed me and wed me might be motivated more by revenge than a quest for respectability,' she said slowly.

Alej almost smiled, until he reminded himself that her sometimes uncanny ability to read his mind was something he should be wary of. It was certainly nothing to admire. Yet her words rang true, didn't they? A marriage of convenience would undoubtedly put paid to the rather tedious description of playboy, which always followed him around. But more than that, it would place her uniquely in his control. They would be living together and sleeping together. What greater opportunity would there be for him to have his delicious fill of her before casting her aside, as once she had done to him? 'It is true that my feelings towards you are mixed, Emily.'

'Because I was the only woman to have ever walked away?' she guessed.

'You think my ego overrides all other considerations?'

'Possibly.'

'I cannot deny your words and yet it is a little more...complex than that, *querida*.' There was a pause. 'You never really gave me a reason for your sudden change of mind, did you, Emily? You went from screaming ecstatically in my arms to condescending ice maiden within the space of hours. You walked away from me as if we were strangers who had just met. You gave me your virginity, then you told me that you didn't love me and that you wanted other men. And you never really explained why.'

There was a pause while Emily's mind spun with possibilities and she stared down at the swirly patterns on her trousers, unwilling to meet his piercing gaze. Surely it was best to just brush his question aside and leave the past where it should be. But then she wondered who she was trying to protect—surely not a man

who had ruled her mother's life with a rod
of steel before leaving his stepdaughter a sick
horse as a final mark of contempt. And wasn't
there a part of Emily which wanted to redeem
herself in Alej's eyes—who wanted him to stop
looking at her with that thinly veiled scorn?

'My stepfather threatened me,' she said
slowly as she lifted her gaze to his. 'He told
me he would never forgive me if I continued
to see you.'

He gave a bitter laugh, shaking his head so
that the dark waves of hair dangled around his
neck. 'And, of course, he was such a worthwhile individual that you desperately needed
his approval? Forgive me if I don't buy that,
Emily, when I know how much you hated and
feared him. Perhaps you were more concerned
he would cut off all your money.'

She sucked in a deep breath as she lifted her
gaze to him. Had she stupidly underestimated
his intelligence? That he would just suck up
any story she was prepared to give him? 'No,
you're right. It wasn't just that,' she admitted
and she swallowed the lump which had risen
in her throat. 'My mother begged me to listen
to him and to do as he said, because he threatened to divorce her if I got involved with someone like you.'

'*Someone like me?*' he repeated. 'What exactly does that mean?'

The lump in her throat wasn't shifting but Emily knew she couldn't avoid the question burning from his green eyes. 'You were poor and had no father and that didn't sit well with his inflated ideas of his place in society. My mother was terrified of what her life without him would be.'

'Without his wealth, you mean?' he suggested softly.

Emily bit her lip. No, not just his wealth—although that had obviously been a big attraction. But her mother had been one of those women for whom a life was not complete without a man. Her first husband had been poor and after being widowed, she had devoted all her energy to finding a rich replacement and, when she'd succeeded, had clung onto him like a limpet.

And didn't it frighten Emily to think she might have inherited that sapping trait of mindless dependence? She'd been acutely aware of loving Alej back then, in a way which could never have been reciprocated—because what hope was there for a relationship between a man on the brink of a glittering international career and a teenager who was barely out of school? Wasn't that another factor which had convinced her it would be better in the long run if she let him go, because that way she would avoid all the inevitable pain when he stopped caring about her? Once again, she dropped her gaze, not wanting him to see the fear in her eyes.

'Something like that,' she said.

Alej stiffened. She was lying about something, he just didn't know what—lying in that smooth, natural way which came so easily to women. But, in a way, didn't her duplicity bolster his intention to wed her? His mouth twisted. Wouldn't it give him a kick to make a mockery out of the whole damned institution of marriage, while allowing him to enjoy legal sex with the woman who could turn him on like nobody else?

'But they divorced anyway, didn't they?' he questioned.

She swallowed. 'Yes.'

'And your mother died soon afterwards?'

She paused for a moment, recounting the facts like bullet points—as if she was determined to avoid having to answer any more questions about it. 'Yes. In a house fire. I was away at university and unable to visit her as often as I'd done before. She'd taken tranquillisers—more than usual—and obviously didn't put out her cigarette properly. She didn't hear the smoke alarm go off and by the time the fire brigade arrived, it was too late. They said she wouldn't have known anything.' For a long time afterwards she had been plagued by guilt. Guilt that she'd been unable to save her mother. And guilt at the relief she'd felt on being freed from the burden of care.

He spoke softly in Spanish, sympathising with her for her loss, and she inclined her head in acceptance.

'Thank you,' she said.

But Alej did not allow the momentary air of reflection to detract him from his purpose as he forged on with his proposal. 'Of course, if you married me—'

She shook her head. 'Alej, let it go. It's not going to happen. Why would it?'

'Why, for sex and for money, of course,' he continued softly. 'Those are the main reasons why women marry rich and eligible men, aren't they? We're just being a little more open about it than most.'

'And what about...' she hesitated before plucking up enough courage to ask it '...what about love?'

'What about it? I think it's overrated.' He saw something die in her eyes and felt a warm rush of pleasure. 'Overused,' he continued, with harsh emphasis. 'And even if you feel it for a while—it's soon over.'

'But there are other kinds of love,' she objected. 'The kind which endures. What about the love a mother has for her child?'

Alej felt his skin grow cold. 'You think your mother was such a shining example of maternal love, do you, Emily?'

She shook her head. 'I'm not naïve enough to think that, no. But maybe your mother—'

'Let's just change the subject, shall we?' he interrupted. 'I thought we were talking about my marriage to you.'

'We were. And I've made my feelings on the subject clear.'

He got out of bed and he could see suspicion vying with desire as he walked over to the window seat and pulled her to her feet. And as soon as she was in his arms, all that instant chemistry was back. The moment they touched—even though he was naked and she was fully dressed—he became fired up with lust.

'Would you like me to change your mind for you?'

'That's not…fair,' she mumbled unconvincingly as he began to stroke his finger over her neck beneath the thick fall of unbrushed hair.

'I think you would,' he murmured. 'That's the feeling I'm getting, loud and clear.'

'We're…we're standing right in front of the window.'

'It's reflective from the outside,' he growled. 'Nobody can see in.'

He silenced any further words with his mouth, finding her lips with an urgent kind of hunger, achingly aware of the low groan which seemed to come from deep inside him. She kissed with a passion which made him silently curse and wonder how she could make him feel this way. Like it was the first time all over again. As if he'd never had sex with anyone else. His groin grew rock-hard and he closed his heart to further analysis. It was what it was. Why knock it before he had fully exploited it?

His hands on her hips, he backed her towards the nearest wall and wondered if this might bring her to her senses. If she'd tell him to get his hands off her and announce she was going to break her contract, because they couldn't keep having indiscriminate sex like this, as boss and employee. And didn't part of him want that? Wouldn't he have respected her more if she'd done that—shown some fire and spirit and strength—if she'd morphed back into the pure virgin he'd once known and respected? But she didn't. She did what every woman who ever came near him did. Flung her arms around his neck and positioned herself with an effortless tilt of her pelvis, so that the removal of her trousers became almost seamless.

Her panties slid to the floor and she bucked as he touched her. He wanted to explode as he moved his hand away from her wet heat to fetch another condom, but the action wasn't made any easier by the frantic way Emily was circling her hips. With a swift, delaying kiss he pushed her away and walked over to find what he was looking for, tearing open the foil as he reached her again. Bending his head to her peaking nipple, he slid one hand between her thighs. He wanted to instruct her to put the rubber on for him, but already he seemed so close to coming that he suspected her trembling fingers might end it all too quickly and the risk of *that* was something he wouldn't tolerate.

It seemed to take for ever, but at last he was able to push deep inside her and the loud groan he heard reverberating around the high-ceilinged room was all his. He rocked into her— over and over—and it was hard and fast and elemental. He heard her choked sob as she began to come but his own orgasm was upon him almost immediately. Swamped by the pulsing tide of pleasure and fatigued by the lethargy which instantly swept over him, he slumped against her, his breath fanning her neck. Long seconds passed—or it might have been minutes—until he had the strength to lift his head to study her. To brush away her ruffled hair as he bent his lips to her ear.

'So. Are you going to marry me, Emily?'

Emily told herself to say no. To protect herself from his powerful allure and from her own weakness and susceptibility to him. But no words came. Only a stupid rush of pleasure at the thought of being his wife. Something painful twisted deep inside her, because she realised that she had walked straight into a trap of her own making. She'd proposed a marriage of convenience because she'd thought it could help advance his political aspirations and, now that the chips were down, she couldn't bear the thought of some other woman wearing his ring.

So could she risk marrying him, despite the fact that once she'd loved him and she suspected that a lot of that love was still there? Because if she agreed to become his bride it was imperative she keep that fact secret, or she would be at a tactical disadvantage. Far better to focus on the material advantages of becoming Señora Sabato and allow Alej to think she was motivated by nothing more threatening than avarice.

'I guess it's too good an offer to turn down,' she said, injecting her voice with a deliberate note of greed.

As if on cue, a cold light flared in his green eyes. 'Of course it is.'

'How much are you offering me?' she continued, forcing herself to play the game. 'How much do you think I'm worth?'

'The two things are not necessarily the same.' A hard light came into his eyes as, slowly, he told her just how much he was prepared to pay.

Emily swallowed, the game momentarily forgotten. 'Gosh,' she said faintly. 'I guess only an idiot would refuse that kind of money.'

'Or someone with principles, perhaps— which have clearly bypassed you along the way,' he responded cuttingly. 'What kind of a wedding do you want, Emily?'

The kind where the groom is looking at me with love, not with a mixture of scorn and lust. The kind which is destined to last for ever.

But Emily pushed the hopeless thoughts away and shrugged, determined not to communicate the sudden hopeless ache in her heart.

'If we're going to go through with a meaning-less ceremony, we might as well do it in style,' she said briskly. 'I mean, I think a church ser-vice would be a step too far, but there's no reason why we can't go the whole hog with a white dress and flowers and all the attendant razzmatazz. That's the kind of story which the press love—and this is all about publicity, isn't it? And in the meantime...' She cleared her throat. 'We really ought to have an engage-ment ring to add credibility.'

He nodded. 'Have a look online in the morn-ing and choose something you like the look of.'

'Online?' she repeated dully.

'Sure. There must be some sort of design you've always lusted after. Carat size no ob-stacle, of course. We should be able to take delivery of it before the big race tomorrow, so that you can show it off to the world.'

Emily's heart pounded. His words were the antithesis of romance but she told herself to be grateful for that. Because nothing could have emphasised better that this was simply a mar-riage of convenience than Alej's emotionless statement about buying her engagement ring online.

CHAPTER EIGHT

THERE WERE FLOWERS EVERYWHERE. Massed white roses and tiny pale-blue forget-me-nots, which Emily quickly realised were the colours of the Argentinian flag. It was a nice touch from the Vinoly Hotel, she acknowledged—a luxury South American–owned hotel in London which Alej had taken over for the weekend and where their wedding was shortly to take place.

She stared into the mirror at the unlikely vision of herself in a wedding dress, because, despite her groom's sarcastic words about choosing the kind of engagement ring she'd always lusted after, she'd never had daydreams about what she might wear on such a day. There had been one very glaring omission to wedding-day dreams because it had been impossible to imagine such a day without Alej, which had obviously been a strictly forbidden fantasy. But fantasy had somehow become reality and a huge yellow-diamond engagement ring was sparkling at her finger, while a waterfall of tulle was held in place by a fragrant crown of creamy roses. Behind her stood Marybeth, though still with concern criss-crossing her face.

'Are you sure?' questioned her only bridesmaid, for the hundredth time. 'It's not too late to back out. I mean, are you absolutely sure you're doing the right thing?'

Of course she wasn't. But Emily certainly couldn't blame her friend for her repeated questioning. Wouldn't she have done exactly the same if the situation had been reversed? Brushing her fingertip over one of the antique roses in her bouquet, she forced a smile. 'Why wouldn't I be?'

'Because it's been so fast—'

'I know. But we were lovers years ago.'

'Yeah. So you said. But *marriage*? Especially when you seemed so unsure about even *taking* the job. And now this. A big, fancy wedding in front of the Argentinian ambassador and all. It's such a big step. Do you…?' Marybeth shifted a little awkwardly on her mauve satin ballet pumps 'Do you love him, Emily?'

Emily felt her heart twist. She didn't want to

answer this—not to herself and certainly not to her closest girlfriend. Because who wasn't to say that the churning emotions she'd been experiencing for weeks weren't just the result of hormones—of her body finally being sexually satisfied after all the arid years since Alej had last made love to her? Yet because she could see the fear on Marybeth's face, she found herself uttering soothing words, which happened to be rooted in truth.

'I...care for him,' she said.

'Okay...' said Marybeth, a little doubtfully. 'Well, that's certainly an improvement on what you were saying about him before you went to Oz. Better get going, then—and get this party started!'

But Emily's nerves felt jangled as she made her way towards the grand function room, despite her smooth words of assurance. She hadn't seen Alej since the day after his shock proposal and had since been beset by a growing fear that he might have changed his mind and simply not shown up. It was only when she'd peeped out of her hotel window that morning, and seen a whole fleet of black limousines arriving, that she'd realised he wasn't planning on reneging on his intention to make her his wife—and she'd been taken aback by the relief which had washed over her.

In order to arrange a fancy wedding at such short notice, she had flown back from Melbourne alone, after Alej's team had—in true fairy-tale tradition—won themselves a podium place at the city's Grand Prix. Afterwards there had been fireworks and champagne and a party which had gone on all night, during which he had announced their surprise engagement to an already febrile press. And amid all the excitement of reporting that one of the world's biggest commitment-phobes was finally taking the plunge into matrimony, Emily realised that her new fiancé's political intentions had very definitely been put on the back burner.

But he had shrugged almost carelessly when she had pointed this out. 'A couple of weeks won't make any difference.'

'Maybe not.' Her voice had grown thoughtful. 'We could announce it while we're on honeymoon. It will be a good press release, especially if we pick a day when there isn't much news around.'

There had been an odd note in his voice. 'You think of everything, don't you, Emily?'

'That's what you're paying me for.'

His voice had mocked her. 'No, *querida*. I'm paying you for a lot more than that.'

It was an observation which caused her some disquiet and one she didn't want to reflect on for too long—but then she'd had a lot of practice at pushing unwanted thoughts away. Life was strange, she thought as the doors of the grand salon swam into view. Hard to believe that in a few minutes' time she would be Alej's wife—something she'd longed for in those far-off days as an impressionable teenager. But this was nothing more than a complex game they were playing—and she should forget that at her peril.

The sound of a string quartet greeted her as one of Alej's hunky polo-playing friends pushed open the ornate doors and as everyone turned to look at her, for a split second, she felt beset by more nerves. She wondered if Alej's friends were judging her and wondering why his standards had fallen so far below his usual diet of supermodels and heiresses. Yet wasn't another part of her secretly wishing this was the real thing, instead of being the ultimate public relations gesture?

But then she saw him waiting for her beneath an arch of flowers and felt her heart hitch beneath the silk-satin of her gown, because he looked utterly gorgeous. The most gorgeous man in the room. Wearing a suit more formal than anything she'd ever seen him in before and, with a couple of centimetres clipped from his ruffled black hair, he appeared to be a more sombre version of the man she'd known in previous guises. His new air of gravitas was slightly unsettling, emphasising again that this was simply a different mask he was wearing. Yet the moment he took her hand in his, all her determination to keep emotion at bay drained away and her heart gave a great big leap of longing.

I don't want to love him, she thought desperately. *I don't want to be hurt by him.*

'You look beautiful,' he said.

It was said presumably to add credibility, but nonetheless his words made Emily glow as she handed her bouquet to Marybeth. 'Thank you,' she said, hiding her excitement behind a calm smile.

The ceremony passed without event and only afterwards did Emily realise she'd been on tenterhooks throughout the entire proceedings. Had she been afraid that his supermodel ex would burst through the doors and try to put a stop to it, like in some dramatic Hollywood film? There was a hush as Alejandro made his vows, his eyes fixed on hers with an expression of desire underpinned with something darker. Something which made her senses scream out a nameless warning, despite the sensual ache which was already starting low in her belly. Because wasn't that hostility she could see flickering in the depths of his steady green gaze?

Afterwards, a starry reception spilled over into an adjoining function room, filled with politicians, actors and even members of the British royal family, with whom Alej used to play polo, back in the day. She thought how easily he mixed in such an elevated section of society and how her own guest list was far more modest—though Marybeth's family certainly made up for any paucity in numbers with their noise and laughter. And then the music began to play for the first dance and, as Alej took her hand and everyone turned towards them, Emily felt as if she was walking onto a giant stage.

Because you are. Because this is all make-believe and none of it is real.

But in that moment it *felt* real as Alej laced his warm fingers in hers and led her onto the dance floor. As achingly familiar strains filtered into her ears, she wondered if he was deliberately torturing her with a song she hadn't heard for many years.

'What made you choose this?' she questioned, the silk of her wedding gown whispering over the marble floor as she tried and failed to erase the blissful memories of those hot, Argentinian nights.

'You used to love it.'

She shifted awkwardly but, annoyingly, it only seemed to decrease the space between them. 'Maybe I did, but not...not any more.'

'No. Your tastes are more sophisticated these days, perhaps?'

'It's not that.' She drew in a deep breath. 'We're not the same people any more, Alej. It doesn't seem appropriate, somehow.'

'What would you rather they played?' He spun her round, his eyes glinting hard and green. '"Money, Money, Money"?'

She didn't react to the taunt. 'Let's try to keep the hostilities to a minimum for the duration of the reception, shall we?'

'Then try smiling, Princesa. Instead of looking as if you're standing on the edge of a deep precipice.'

'And if I told you that was exactly how I felt?'

His eyes bored into her. 'And why might that be?'

She hesitated. 'Because I'm finding this all harder than I imagined it would be.'

'Why?'

'I don't *know*!'

Three beats of music followed and Alej tightened his fingers around her waist, because it was the first time she'd let that cool mask of composure slip and inexplicably he found himself wanting to see what was behind it. 'Do you miss your family?' he questioned suddenly. 'Do you wish your mother was here today?'

She tilted her head back and he could see her throat constrict, and the tiny pearl which hung from the end of a fine gold chain quivered at her neck.

'Yes,' she admitted, her voice breaking a little, her free hand reaching up to touch the necklace. 'It's stupid, but I do. She was a terrible mother in many ways but she was still my mother.'

'Is that her necklace?'

She nodded. 'My father bought it for her before they were married. She hardly ever wore it—said it was too cheap—but I love it. Far more than any of those flashy jewels which Paul bought her and which she ended up pawning anyway.'

Alej felt a wave of something approaching sympathy until he quickly reined it back in. He didn't *want* to feel sympathy for her. He wanted to feel only the things he could deal with—like lust and anger and the hot, sweet release of fulfilment. Because she'd never given a *damn* about him and his family, had she? Never even stopped to find out what had happened to his mother. His lying, cheating mother, but—as she herself had just said— his mother all the same. His mouth twisted. Of course she hadn't. Because the little people were invisible to people like Emily. She might have affected to despise her snobbish stepfa- ther, but maybe she'd absorbed more of his values than she'd been aware of.

He put his lips close to her neck, his voice growing husky. 'I'm bored with dancing and bored with people watching our every move. How soon before we can escape so that I can consummate this marriage of ours, because I am aching for you, Emily? Can you feel how much?'

'We can't...' Her words tailed off as he slid his thigh between hers. 'We can't just leave the reception early in order to go to bed.'

'Why not?'

'Because that's not playing the game we're

supposed to be playing,' she said sternly, her voice taking on a note of firmness. 'We have to at least *look* as if we love each other, even if it isn't true—otherwise the marriage will appear to be a stunt instead of looking authentic, and that could easily backfire on you.'

'So how would you like me to manifest my "love" towards you, Emily?' he taunted, pleased to see her cheeks flush a deep pink in response to his swirling movement, which was making his hardened pelvis thrust against the slippery silk of her wedding gown.

'We could try having a conversation, rather than making out on the dance floor.'

He bit back a reluctant smile. 'What do you want to talk about?'

Her fingers curled against his chest, her hand a pale starfish against the dark material of his suit jacket, and he found himself covering it with his own.

'What we're going to do for our honeymoon, for a start.'

With an effort, he dragged his thoughts away from the sensation of her breasts pushing against his torso, which was resulting in a punishing hardness in his groin. 'I told you,' he said. 'We take my plane wherever you want to go and stay in five-star luxury along the way.'

'Not the best idea.' She shook her head. 'I think that will be counter-productive.'

'Meaning?'

'It will continue to make you look like some aimless playboy with more money than he knows what to do with and no general purpose in life.'

'You may or may not be aware that wherever in the world I am, I work—and I work hard,' he said coldly. 'It is possible to do such things remotely these days.'

'I know it is. But there will be no real focus for me, will there?' She shrugged and seemed to find it difficult to meet his eyes. 'It'll just be all about…sex.'

'It's a honeymoon, Emily,' he pointed out.

'But not a real one,' she reminded him sharply.

'Are you telling me you're unhappy about the idea of having wall-to-wall sex? That's certainly not the impression you've given me so far.'

'That's not what I'm saying at all. But I'm still going to be working for you—and when we decide to call time on the marriage, I want to have achieved what I set out to achieve. Call it professional pride, if you like.' She waited until the Argentinian ambassador had danced past them with a complicated sashay of his hips. 'Do you remember my original brief to you in Melbourne?'

'I've scarcely thought of anything else,' he said sardonically.

'When we talked about simplifying your life, you decided to sell off your home in France because, if you're planning to be based in Argentina, it makes no sense for you to have a base in Paris. So couldn't we…couldn't we use the honeymoon to go there—and afterwards maybe go to your *estancia*?'

'Why?'

Because although I know it's a kind of madness, I want to see some of the different facets of your life. I want to glimpse the private man behind the glossy façade. I want to see your homes—not just the fancy and impersonal five-star hotels you seem to spend your life in.

But Emily had no intention of revealing her foolish thoughts to him, so instead she gave a careless shrug. 'It might be an idea to choose whichever sentimental items you want to keep before your Parisian apartment goes on the market. It might be very satisfying to tidy your life up like that.'

'I can think of only one thing which will satisfy me right now,' he growled. 'And it has nothing to do with the marketing of property and everything to do with the removal of your clothes.'

'Alej Sabato! You are outrageous!'

But he paid her half-hearted protest no heed, dancing her smoothly out of the ballroom and into the discreet elevator, which had exclusive access to the hotel's newly designed honeymoon suite. The elevator doors had barely slid shut before he pushed her up against a rose-tinted mirror, his hand sliding inside the bodice of her wedding gown as he started to kiss her.

'People will notice we've gone,' she gasped against his urgent mouth, as, blindly, he jabbed at the top-floor button with his finger.

'Who cares? We're married, Emily. This is legal.'

There was champagne on ice and roses everywhere but the moment their suite door swung closed, their only focus was on pulling at each other's clothes. His suit hit the deck and her wedding dress lay abandoned on the carpet and soon they were naked on the great big honeymoon bed—save for the coronet of roses still pinned in her hair.

Emily could see her wedding ring glinting gold as Alejandro pulled her into his arms, his eyes a blaze of green as he began to plunder her mouth once more. 'Oh,' she said breathlessly, as his hand slid searchingly over every naked curve, his unsteady survey of her flesh making it feel as if he were discovering her by touch alone. As if it were an eternity since they'd lain together rather than a matter of days. His name trembled on her lips. 'Alej.'

'Shh…'

Afterwards she was glad he had quietened her because hadn't she felt a compelling urge to tell him how much she'd missed him during their days apart—and if she started indulging in that kind of revelation, who knew where it might end? So she kissed him hard instead, mounting her own survey of the flat planes of his magnificent physique—perfect save for the jagged scar on his back, which he had refused to discuss. Her orgasm came quickly—powerfully intense as it racked through her body in a way which made her feel momentarily helpless. Did her choked mewl of fulfilment touch something inside him? Was that why his arms tightened around her and he buried his face in her hair before groaning out his own shuddering pleasure?

She must have fallen asleep, because when she opened her eyes again, it was to see early stars already beginning to pepper the sky outside the un-shuttered windows. Still sleepy and caught in the half-world between wakefulness and slumber, her mind drifted around tantalising pathways. Was it possible they could make this marriage work? she wondered fleetingly. Could they compromise somehow? Forget about the bad stuff and concentrate on the good stuff and learn to love one another all over again?

'Are you awake?' she whispered.

'I am now.' Alej rolled over and studied her. Awake and already hard and wanting more—for that was the effect she had on him. *The effect she'd always had on him.* He ran his fingers over her pale and quivering body, watching her nipples harden as he scratched his nails lightly over the soft fuzz of hair at her groin, before dipping his head to it.

'Alej?' she said, in a voice which sounded slurred although he knew she had drunk nothing stronger than water at the reception.

'I'm not in the mood for conversation right now,' he ground out.

He parted her thighs gently and began to minister to her with his mouth, hearing her moan as he slowly licked her damp folds. He flicked the tip of his tongue against her tight bud, enjoying her unique taste and the way her nails scrabbled helplessly at the petal-strewn duvet as he quickened the movement. And in a moment of disturbing clarity, he realised he had only ever done this with her. It had been just one of the myriad ways they had pleasured each other without the actual act of penetration, when she had been so young. The memory of that had stayed stubbornly with him and the thought of laying his mouth so intimately against another woman had repulsed him. Yet even that simple fact had maddened him, for he saw it as a weakness and unwanted dependence upon the woman who had rejected him. He wanted to draw his mouth away in order to frustrate her but instead he found himself revelling in the taste of her. Musk and honey, he thought achingly, and he hardened as she began convulsing against his lips.

There was another condom close by but, although he was rock-hard and eager to enter her, something held him back. Instead, he watched until her shuddered breathing had steadied itself and then her eyelids fluttered open, as if she had suddenly become aware that his gaze was on her. He saw the trace of uncertainty which crossed her face and for some reason that gave him pleasure as he lay back against the bed and, with a careless flick of his hand, indicated the throbbing hardness at his groin.

'Now you,' he said softly. 'Your turn.'

Still dazed after her orgasm, Emily felt suddenly wary about what he wanted her to do, yet surely that was completely illogical. After all, she'd done it many times in the past—not just in the stables but outside in the lush pastures, where the fresh Argentinian air had helped provide her with a liberating sense of freedom. But back then they had been *close*. Young and passionate—with none of all the bad history or hang-ups which had stood between them like a barrier ever since. Suddenly she felt almost *shy* about what he wanted her to do—and she needed to lose that attitude quickly. She was a grown-up, she reminded herself. And now a wife.

So she wriggled down the bed to position her head close to his groin, running light fingertips over his erect shaft and registering the instinctive shudder which racked through his body as she did so. Up and down, her thumb and forefinger moved with feather-light touch, revelling in the sensation of his silk-encased hardness. She continued with this stealthy rhythm until she saw his eyelids flutter to a close, and only when she was sure she wasn't

being observed did she bend her head to him.
He moaned as she took him into her mouth
and already she could feel the sticky wetness
on his tip as she began to suck him.

'Emily,' he groaned, tangling his fingers
into her hair and dislodging a stray clip from
her bridal headdress, which he plucked out and
tossed to the floor.

She danced her tongue over him, tracing little patterns over his pulsing stiffness, enjoying the way he thrust his pelvis towards her,
as if silently begging for relief. But Alej didn't
beg, she reminded herself. He'd told her that
a long time ago. She opened her mouth wider
because he had suddenly tensed and she felt a
rush of something like triumph as he flooded
into her mouth. She revelled in the salty taste
of him as she raised her head and drew the tip
of her tongue over her lips to catch a drop she
must have missed, realising that he was watching her intently.

But it wasn't satisfaction she could read in
the suddenly stony depths of his eyes, but a
dark anger she'd never seen there before. She
blinked at him in confusion, feeling out of her
depth. 'You didn't enjoy that?'

'Don't ask disingenuous questions. You
know damned well I did.'

Her confusion deepened. 'Then why aren't you smiling?'

'Because I have something on my mind. Do you want to know what it is?'

Actually, she didn't, because she suspected she wasn't going to like it—but she wasn't a child who could simply run away from things which might be hard to hear. 'Go ahead,' she said quietly.

Crossing his arms behind his head, he pillowed his head on his elbows. 'I'd forgotten just how good you were at doing that. But as you were licking and sucking me with such beautiful precision, I couldn't help but wonder how many other men you have administered to in such a way.'

Administered to in such a way? Emily recoiled with something like indignation. He was making her sound like some sort of perverted nurse! 'You're asking me to tell you how many men I've slept with?' she questioned.

He looked momentarily surprised at her candour before quickly recovering himself, but Emily reminded herself that Alej Sabato didn't have the monopoly on being 'blunt'. And wasn't this something which needed to come out anyway? Hadn't it troubled her for a long time that the erroneous picture she'd once painted of herself was one she deeply regretted?

His voice was harsh. 'That's exactly what I'm asking you.'

'None,' she said flatly.

He shifted his position slightly, his eyes narrowing. 'Excuse me?'

'None,' she repeated. 'Would you like me to say it in Spanish for you? *Ninguno!* You're the only man I've ever given oral sex to! The only man I've ever been intimate with! The only one! Do you understand? I told you I wanted to have sex with other men because it was the only way I could guarantee you wouldn't come after me. I knew it would disgust you and I was right. But I did it because I thought it was for the best all round. I honestly didn't think we had any kind of future together, Alej.'

Alej sat up, his heart pounding as the meaning of her words sank into his disbelieving ears. She hadn't slept with another man in eight long years? Could she be speaking the truth? His gaze swept over her. Her cheeks were flushed, her long fair hair ruffled from where he'd been running his fingers through it and her lips darkened by the pressure of his kisses. On the one hand he was pleased—of course he was—because the thought of her so intimately touching another man was like plunging a dagger deep into his heart.

But on the other…

Anger began to well up inside him, like the slow swell of the ocean when a storm was approaching. Because wasn't this the greatest sin of all—the one committed by every woman he had ever known?

'So when you told me that you wanted other men,' he questioned, his voice unsteady, 'that you had seen other, more *suitable* men…'

She shook her head as his words tailed off. 'It wasn't true. You were the only man I ever wanted,' she breathed. 'The only one I could ever contemplate being intimate with. You still are.'

Alej felt a punch of primitive satisfaction but forced himself to ignore it, because sexual exclusivity wasn't really what he was focused on, no matter how much it pleased him to realise that he was the only one. Because she was missing the point completely. She was looking at him as if he should be pleased. As if she'd just given him some kind of gift instead of reinforcing the most bitter truth of all. And the most stupid thing of all was why he had thought she was any different from all the rest.

Because all women lied, didn't they? His

mother had lied to him and then Colette had lied *about* him, but, for some reason, the false-hoods which had sprung from Emily's lips had been the hardest of all to bear.

And still he didn't know what to believe.

'So were you lying to me then?' he questioned softly. 'Or are you lying to me now?'

CHAPTER NINE

THEY FLEW TO France the very next morning, to Alej's apartment in the eighth arrondissement—a sprawling affair at the top of an historic building, situated on a famous street, opposite an equally famous hotel. In the distance the River Seine glinted in the sunshine, and nearby the trees in the Tuileries Garden provided a leafy canopy for wandering young lovers.

But not for her and Alej, Emily reflected a couple of days later, as she looked around at the lavish but unlived-in surroundings of her husband's Parisian home. They might have been photographed together walking around the city's famously romantic spots, but it had all been for show. A sham. Just like their marriage.

It made her shudder to think she'd been naively wondering if maybe they could make a go of their marriage, but never again would she be guilty of allowing herself to believe in such an illusion. Why would she when, in Alej's eyes, she had committed the cardinal sin of lying and he could not—or would not—forgive her for the transgression she had owned up to on the first night of their honeymoon. The memory of it still jarred. It sat like a black cloud on her horizon. He'd accused her of being a liar and she had no defence against his words because they had been true. She *had* pretended not to care for him and to want other men. But when she'd tried to explain her reasons— maybe even to express all the love and fear which had motivated her actions—his clipped command had cut her short.

'A lie is just that, Emily,' he had drawled. 'There can be no justification. And women lie as easily as breathing. Fact.'

She tried not to care and to throw herself into the role she was being paid for, because surely that should now be her priority. She liaised with his assistant about their travel plans and arranged an in-depth interview with one of France's most respected journals, in which Alejandro talked with passion about polo. About how the sport had rescued him from poverty and that he wanted more children to benefit from similar opportunities.

Sitting in on the interview, Emily had been

confused about why he wasn't promoting his burgeoning political career, but didn't dare butt in and prompt him, though she might have done if it had been anyone else. And when the interviewer suddenly asked whether he planned on having children himself now that he was married, Alej had glanced up at Emily, his gaze hard and impenetrable.

'No plans at present,' he had replied smoothly.

And Emily had despaired at the stab of pain which shafted through her as she'd heard those words, as once again she'd found herself longing to hold a baby against her breast and to suckle the child of Alej Sabato. Dragging her thoughts back to the present, she turned away from the window, away from the glitter of the upmarket shops and the silver gleam of the river. What a hopeless fool she was.

Only at night did her new husband let his guard down, when an unspoken truce left no room for anything other than mutual delight under cover of darkness. But even then Emily wasn't safe from her own stupid, see-sawing emotions. Because when they were naked and he was kissing her and moaning out his pleasure, it was all too easy to get carried away. To imagine he felt something other than carnal desire for her. But he didn't. He couldn't have made that plainer. She was his temporary wife who served a dual purpose in life. Who provided him with respectability and sex. And wouldn't she have been a hypocrite if she had refused the latter through some kind of warped principle, when she enjoyed it just as much as he did?

They spent several days in the city, trawling through his personal effects while Alej selected items he wished to keep, but there were surprisingly few. A scale model of one of his racing cars. A bronze sculpture of his first polo pony and a framed paparazzi photo of the US president sipping from a can of MiMaté. Everything else—the contemporary furniture, the stunning artwork and a small library of rare edition books—he had dismissed with a careless flick of his fingers.

'Get rid of them. I don't want them.'

'Is there anything of Colette's here, which she might have forgotten to take?' She cleared her throat and forged on. 'Perhaps she…she might want to come and pick something up?'

His smile was knowing, as if he was perfectly aware that her question was a thinly disguised method of gathering information. For a moment she wondered if he was about to withhold it, but, with a look of mockery, he supplied it.

'Colette never actually lived here, even though she liked to make out she did. There's nothing of hers here and little else that interests me. So auction it all off. The money raised can go to my charitable foundation.'

Emily supposed it was an admirable way to dispose of his past, if a little cold-blooded.

'And in case you're wondering,' he continued silkily, 'Colette now lives in New York, so it's unlikely you're going to run into her along the Avenue Montaigne.'

Emily found herself expelling a huge sigh of relief because she'd actually been dreading bumping into the glamorous supermodel. Was it that or the fact that their time in Paris was drawing to a close which made her suddenly dare to try to open up some further lines of communication between them? Or because they'd gone to bed soon after lunch and his defences were down? He had seemed very much like the Alej of old as he had explored her body and lazily kissed every inch of her skin and she had found herself revelling in their old familiarity and wishing she could deepen it.

She could hear the sound of the shower being turned off and minutes later he walked into the bedroom, a white towel wrapped around his narrow hips and tiny droplets of water highlighting the honed perfection of his olive skin. She watched his reflection in the mirror. The liquorice-black tendrils of his hair were damp, his buttocks were paler than the dark skin above and below—and wasn't it predictable that she could feel her body instantly respond, despite the fact that they'd been having non-stop sex all afternoon?

He opened the wardrobe door, giving her a perfect view of that livid scar on his back—a scar he now seemed comfortable about letting her see, though there had still been no explanation about how he'd acquired it. But everyone had scars, Emily realised suddenly. Just not all of them were visible.

In a couple of hours' time they were meeting a friend of his from way back, an Italian businessman named Salvatore di Luca who was bringing along his latest girlfriend—a neuroscientist who happened to look like an underwear model—which was probably why Emily had allowed Alej to buy her a dress from the Chanel shop, which was situated just along the street from his apartment. She was wearing it now and the deceptively simple cut of the fine black silk was ridiculously flattering, as were the killer heels which were sitting beside the door to be put on at the last possible moment. But her appearance was the last thing on her mind. Suddenly she knew that she wasn't prepared to be fobbed off with throwaway answers any more. She didn't care if this relationship of theirs wasn't destined to last— why *shouldn't* she learn as much as she could about the man with whom she was temporarily spending her life?

She waited until he was almost dressed, because his nakedness was distracting, and then she turned from where she'd been seated at the dressing table, applying a light slick of lipstick.

'Are you ever going to tell me how you got that scar?' she questioned.

He shrugged as he tugged up the zip on his suit trousers. 'I told you I didn't want to talk about it.'

'I know you did. But I do.'

His eyes narrowed. 'Why?'

'Because we're about to have dinner with one of your oldest friends and, unless you want him to guess this is a sham marriage, it might be better if you didn't come over as a complete stranger to me.'

'And telling you how I got this thing will help?'

'I think so. It might help explain some of a past which you seem determined to keep hidden.'

He turned around, the movement seeming slow, his green eyes hard and flinty as they surveyed her.

'Please, Alej,' she added quietly.

There was a pause. A long pause. And then he gave a long and ragged sigh. 'I was attacked,' he said finally. 'By a man with a razor. Or, to be more accurate—by several men.'

He saw her flinch, as if a steel blade had penetrated *her* tender flesh. Her fingers flew up to her lips in shock and she looked about eighteen again.

'Oh, my God,' she breathed. 'What happened?'

He wondered afterwards what made him continue with his story because he'd never told anyone else. Was it the afterglow of the delicious sex they'd recently shared? Or because living with someone was way more intimate than he'd anticipated, with the inevitable erosion of all the barriers you tried to erect around yourself?

Or maybe it was simply because it was Emily and she had always been the one to burrow beneath his skin.

And suddenly he was right back there. A different time and a different place. And a very different man. He unlocked the memory and it floated free.

'I'd been playing in Argentina and my team had won the last match of the season, as we were expected to do,' he began slowly. 'I even scored the winning goal.'

'That must have been a good feeling,' she said.

He gave a bitter laugh. 'Not really. I'd been approached to fix that match, but, like every other time it had happened, I'd refused.' There was a pause as he looked at her. 'But the offer still left a bad taste in my mouth and it added to my growing disenchantment with some aspects of the sport.'

She nodded, but she didn't speak. She was an astute woman, he acknowledged—one who had learned to use silence to her own advantage. Because he could have stopped the story there. Told her he'd had a few drinks and got into a fight but didn't bother reporting it because he didn't want the negative press of some barroom brawl. Explained how he'd found a backstreet medic to suture it for him on the quiet—hence the resulting scar. All these things were true, and Alej was a man with a powerful aversion to lies. But there had been other reasons for him not wanting the truth behind the brawl to emerge, hadn't there? He wondered if it was the soft expression in Emily's deep blue eyes which made him want to confide in her, or the sudden realisation that some secrets were so dark that they had the power to eat away at your very soul, if you let them.

'I was in a bar,' he continued. 'A rough, simple kind of place not far from where I'd grown up, where a man can go unbothered and drink his beer in peace.' But it hadn't been like that. Word had got out that he was there and someone had come to find him. The oily thug in the cheap suit Alej had recognised instantly. His face had been ugly with anger, his words uglier still. 'I was approached by a man,' he said, his eyes fixed unblinkingly on Emily's face. 'The same guy who'd tried to get me to fix the match. He blamed me for refusing and for all the money he'd lost as a result. And then he told me that my mother was nothing but a cheap hooker and that he'd "had" her.'

She flinched again, but this time a dull red flush stained her cheeks and he saw the way she clenched her hands into tiny fists. 'How dare he say that?'

He almost smiled at the fervour of her instant denial because hadn't he felt exactly the same, when for a few foolish and naïve moments he'd thought the man was lying? 'He even tried to explain how and where, in very graphic detail, and that's when I hit him.'

'Good! I'm glad you hit him. He deserved it!'

Another sigh left Alej's lungs. The crack of bone and the pliant dip of giving flesh had satisfied him, but only for a moment. Nothing ever lasted for longer than a moment, he reflected bitterly. 'And that's when two of his gorillas came charging in, picked me up and carried me out of there and nobody tried to stop them. And behind that bar, in a dark and stinking alley, they each took turns to trace patterns on my back with a rusty blade, so I would never forget them.'

'Oh, Alej.' She jumped to her feet and scooted towards him, the earnestness on her face seeming at odds with the unusual glamour of her new black dress as she put her arms around him. 'Get off,' he bit out from between gritted teeth as he tried to shake her away.

But still she held him, rubbing at his shoulders as if he had just come in, frozen from the snow. 'No, I won't get off,' she said fiercely. 'You let me touch you whenever we're having sex—well, maybe I want to touch you now, when you need my sympathy.'

'I don't need your damned sympathy,' he

growled, dislodging himself from her grip at last, despite her objections.

'I'll be the judge of that. Please, Alej. Tell me what happened.'

He walked over to the window and watched as an enormous vintage Rolls-Royce pulled up outside the Ritz hotel opposite. 'I left polo the very next day.'

'Why?' she questioned quietly.

He didn't answer for a moment and when he did his words sounded as if they'd been dipped in some corrosive liquid. 'Like I said, I'd been growing disenchanted for some time and the blade attack was the last straw. The cuts those men inflicted on me took a long time to heal— which meant it would be even longer before I could get back to match fitness. And I'd had a severe life shock in learning that my mother was a prostitute. I needed something different to think about. A new direction. And so I left the sport which had devoured my every waking thought for as long as I could remember and went into business instead.'

'And no one stopped to question why?'

She was a public relations officer, Alej reminded himself—of course that would be the first thing she thought of. He turned away from the window and stared at her. 'No. There were no more matches and it was nearly Christmas. I took myself off to the Caribbean to recover and people just thought I was recuperating. It was while I was there that I got an email from the guy who had come up with the idea of the MiMaté drink, asking if I wanted to invest some money in his venture, and, seamlessly, my business career was born.' His mouth twisted. 'And ironically I discovered that fame—or notoriety—still had me in its clutches. That making vast amounts of money breeds its own kind of celebrity.'

'And that was the end of it?' she persisted. 'You weren't scared of being attacked again?'

He shook his head. 'I took courses in martial arts. I learned how to protect myself. Put it this way—I never went into a backstreet bar ever again.'

'And did you talk to your mother?' she questioned slowly. 'About the accusations?'

She was looking puzzled and Alej wondered if she guessed he was holding something back or whether he was crediting her with more astuteness than she actually possessed. But even though he was still questioning his sanity in having started all this, he knew he was going to complete the story. Because wasn't it a relief to let it out at last—like a bitter and poisonous mix which had been living inside him for too long, before finally bubbling to the surface?

'No. It isn't an easy subject to bring up, when you stop to think about it. So I just buried it. Deep.' His voice was rough as he pushed out the words from lungs which suddenly felt dry. 'You see, after my mother was sacked by your stepfather, she never worked again. I'd bought her a little house in the country and she grew vegetables and for a while she seemed almost happy. But then she was diagnosed with lung cancer. She had a full-time carer living with her, and I used to visit her regularly.' He paused and then nodded. 'And even though I'd told myself countless times it couldn't possibly be true, I couldn't shake off the look on that man's face when he told me about her. I kept telling myself it was none of my business. That how she had lived her life was nothing to do with me. I planned to say nothing and then, the day before she died, she turned to me and said, "You know, don't you?"'

He saw incomprehension and then shock on Emily's face. 'She guessed?'

He nodded.

'What did you say?' she breathed.

'I asked her what she meant.'

You know what I mean, son. Her failing

voice had come out as a reedy rasp. *I've seen the empty expression in your eyes whenever you look at me that was never there before. Did you find out that I worked the streets when you were a little boy?*

'And?'

He'd almost forgotten Emily was there. Alej's vision cleared as he met her sapphire gaze. 'What could I say? What could I tell her, other than the truth, when the truth was the only thing I could hold onto? And then she told me everything.' His lips hardened as he spoke and suddenly he got an acrid taste in his mouth. He walked from the bedroom into the dining room, aware of Emily following him, before going over to the antique cabinet which would shortly be sold at auction and pouring two fingers of whisky into a crystal tumbler. He swallowed a fiery mouthful before holding his glass aloft. 'Want one?'

She shook her head. 'No, thanks. I want you to carry on with your story.'

He gave a bitter smile as he put the glass down on the gleaming wood. 'Hers was a not unusual tale and in many ways, I wasn't making a moral judgement. You don't have to stand on a street corner to sell sex for money—I know women who would promise pretty much anything if they thought they were going to get a diamond necklace out of it. But this was a very different version of reality from the one I'd been given when I was growing up.'

Her voice was tentative. 'Surely you wouldn't have expected her to tell you the truth when you were a little boy?'

'Of course not. I could understand why she would keep her prostitution a secret. She wasn't the first young woman who would use her body to pay the bills and she certainly won't be the last,' he bit out. 'But not why she felt the need to lie about the circumstances of my conception and about my father. When we moved from the favela and she found a job as housekeeper to your stepfather, she told me we wouldn't be there long. She explained that my father was a rich and powerful man and one day he would return and rescue us and take us away from a life of servitude and we would live together happily on the acres of the pampas he called home.'

'And you believed her?'

'Of course I did! Children tend to believe what their mothers tell them. And we both know what good liars women can be, don't we, Emily?' There was a pause as he flicked her a cynical look. 'But she saved the best for last. The dramatic deathbed declaration which can never be challenged once the final breath has been taken. There was no rich and powerful papa. No father at all, as it happened—just a former client of hers, an itinerant rogue who used to beat her up.' He swallowed. 'But still she let him keep coming back for more. He was nothing but a thief and a con man who spent most of his time in prison and was killed by wrapping his motorbike round a tree—but not before making her pregnant with another child.'

'Oh, Alej. That's terrible,' said Emily dazedly, blinking her eyelids rapidly as if she was trying to hold back tears. 'I'm so sorry.'

He gave another bitter smile. 'Funny, isn't it? I always regretted being an only child, except then I discovered I wasn't. That I have a younger brother. A child she had no hope of supporting, so she did what any self-respecting mother would do and sold him.'

'What was that you said?' Her voice sounded as if it were coming from a long way away as she stared at him in disbelief. 'Are you telling me your mother had another baby and she *sold it*?'

His jaw firmed. 'That's exactly what I'm telling you.'

'Oh, Alej—'

'No,' he said bitterly. 'Please spare me the kindness and compassion—the trembling lips and big, wet eyes. That's not why I told you. And that's it. That's the story. There is no more.'

'There must be.' She walked over to the drinks cabinet and stood next to him, the delicate silk of her black dress making a soft, whispering sound and the faint scent of summer flowers drifting in the air as she reached him. 'You have a brother, Alej. It may not be the ideal scenario—but that's a wonderful thing, surely? You've got a sibling—which is more than I do. Someone whose gene pool you share. Someone you can have a unique relationship with. Have you managed to find him?'

'No.' Even Alej could hear how cold his voice sounded as he answered her question, but it wasn't nearly as cold as his heart. 'I haven't found him because I haven't bothered looking for him. He was sold to a woman in America and that's all I know.'

'But surely you—'

'There is no "surely" about it,' he ground out. 'I'm too old to believe in fairy stories, Emily. Do you really think I would track him down, so that we could have some great big family reunion? Do you honestly think he knows the background of the woman who gave birth to him? Even if he does, do you imagine that's something he's ever going to want to celebrate?'

Emily didn't answer. Not straight away. Her head was too busy buzzing with the emotional repercussions of his shocking revelation. But one thing quickly became apparent—like the agitated and muddy water of a pond which finally grew still, so you were able to see the stones on the bottom. No wonder Alej was so cold and mistrusting. No wonder he thought all women lied. Because in his experience, they did. She'd told him lies herself, hadn't she? Big, powerful lies. She'd told him she didn't want him. That she'd wanted other men. She'd said that because she was scared—scared of her own feelings and her mother's unpredictable behaviour. Scared of being hurt and scared of the future.

Even now, she'd only given him half the truth, hadn't she? She had been too much of a coward to take that final step and to tell him what was deep in her heart. And didn't he need to hear that, now, when he was at his most vulnerable? When he must be aching and hurting deep inside, despite the proud expression on his face.

'I also need to tell you something, Alej.'

He withered her with a sardonic look. 'Don't tell me your mother was a hooker, too?'

She didn't respond to the jibe. 'When I told you on our wedding day there had been no other man—'

'It had conveniently slipped your mind that you might have forgotten to mention one or two?' he suggested.

She blanked his harsh sarcasm, because of course he would lash out at her—wouldn't anyone have lashed out in the circumstances? But he hadn't yet made sense of his past, she realised—and maybe in a way, she had been guilty of the same. 'No. There has been no other man because...' she swallowed '...because nobody ever came close to you. And what I felt for you, I've... I've never felt for anyone else.'

She didn't know what kind of reaction she had been expecting from this tentative revelation but it certainly wasn't the one she got. All his icy composure had vanished and his face now blazed with sudden fury. 'Is this pity you dole out to me now, Emily?' he demanded savagely, angry green fire spitting from the depths of his eyes. 'You think that because I have revealed my shameful parentage to you, I will grab at any crumb of affection which comes my way? That the illegitimate son of a hooker and a thief will be grateful for anything he can get?'

She saw his pain and his anger and thanked whichever self-protective instinct had stopped her from coming right out and telling him she loved him. And wouldn't logic rather than emotion serve her better than anything else right now? 'I don't care about your past!' she said quietly. 'I don't care who your father was or what your mother did.'

His face was a mask. 'I didn't tell you because I wanted your affirmation,' he said coolly. 'I only told you because you asked.'

CHAPTER TEN

'THE THING IS, ALEJ—if you're serious about going into politics, there are a couple of issues you really need to consider first.'

Alej glanced up from the financial journal which was dancing unintelligibly before his eyes. Emily was standing on the other side of the room, pulling on a pair of silk panties, her curvy body illuminated by the morning sunlight, which was turning her hair to pure gold. He swallowed down the lust which was rising up inside him, a lust which seemed permanently outside his control. Last night before dinner he'd told her his dirty secret, expecting...what? He wasn't sure—but it certainly hadn't been her steadfast acceptance of the grim facts about his parentage as they'd come spilling out of him like dark poison.

He felt his gut twist. He'd thought that knowledge of his past would drive her away.

That he'd see her face contort with disgust, no matter how much she tried to keep it hidden. But instead she had remained calm. There had been no recriminations. No hurt expression at the way he had snapped at her. She'd just slid her feet into her new shoes and they'd gone out for dinner with Salvatore di Luca and his girlfriend and Emily had settled easily into her role of glowing newly-wed. She'd acted as if he hadn't told her the sordid truth about his past, which had only reinforced his prejudices about her. Because maybe now she knew the whole truth about him, she imagined she was in a stronger bargaining position. His jaw tightened. Had she been seduced by the private jets and luxury hotels, the jewels and designer clothes he had provided for her—and decided she didn't want to give them up without a fight? Was her love of material comfort greater than discovering that her husband was the son of a violent drunk and a prostitute?

Yet when they'd had sex last night, she'd been as tender as ever he'd known her. She had held him tightly afterwards, her long fingers gently stroking through his hair in a way which had felt delicious. Dangerously delicious. He had pulled away from her afterwards and had lain there staring mutinously at the darkened ceiling. Was all that tenderness born out of compassion? he had wondered bitterly. Did she really think he needed her *sympathy*?

'Alej?' she was saying. 'Have you been listening to a word I've been saying?'

He shrugged. 'It's not particularly easy to concentrate on anything when you're doing a reverse striptease in front of me,' he drawled.

She was zipping up the sleek cream dress, which had also come from the Chanel shop, and he could see the sudden look of courage which crossed her face—as if she was about to say something he didn't want to hear. 'If you're serious about going into politics,' she said quietly, 'aren't you worried that some of the stuff about your mother will come out?'

Half regretting his impetuousness in telling her, Alej shook his head. 'Why should it? It never has before, not even when I announced I was leaving polo.' His jaw tightened. 'I suspect most of her clients will be dead by now and those who aren't are hardly going to boast about consorting with a prostitute, are they? Even if they do make the connection.'

'But it might,' she persisted. 'Especially if you're entering politics, when every aspect of your past will be dragged into the daylight and raked over.'

He shifted uncomfortably. 'That's just a risk I'm going to have to take.'

'Unless you take control of it,' she suggested.

His eyes narrowed. 'Meaning, what?'

She seemed to choose her words with care. 'None of us should be defined by the things our parents have done. You are a good man, Alej, and you do good things. You have a charitable foundation—'

'Like I told you before, I'm not asking for your affirmation,' he said harshly.

'And rather than living with the fear of disclosure,' she continued firmly, 'I want you to think about making some kind of announcement. If the information about your past comes from you, then it loses some of its power. I'm not suggesting you do it straight away—just think about it when you're about to launch your campaign.'

Once again Alej felt the sharp prick of conscience. He wished she would stop being so damned reasonable, because with each second that passed he was reminded of what had made him fall for her in the first place. Her softness. Her understanding. Her enthusiasm. But that was then, he reminded himself grimly, and this was now. It wasn't going to be easy to do what he had to do and the longer this quasi-marriage went on, the harder it became. But he couldn't give her up. Not yet. There was still too much of her soft sensuality for him to experience before that day came around. He swallowed. So maybe he should take her back to Argentina—to where it all began. To be alone with her and enjoy her over and over again, until his appetite was finally sated. Wouldn't there be a delicious sense of irony to complete the circle that way?

Pushing back the rumpled sheet, he got out of bed. 'I'm having new flight plans drawn up with my pilot,' he said.

'Oh?'

'We're heading for Argentina,' he supplied coolly.

Pausing mid-brush of her hair, she turned round from the mirror and blinked at him. 'Already?'

He shrugged. 'Why not? We're done here in Paris. Make sure you're packed and ready to go. We'll be leaving this afternoon.'

Emily turned away, determined to hide her hurt at his cold and commanding tone, just as she had hidden it yesterday when he had rejected her attempts to comfort him after he'd told her about his mother. But what had she expected—that a man so deeply scarred and traumatised by his terrible past would turn around and let her get close, just like that? Was she really that naïve?

But she refused to do what she suspected Alej wanted her to do—to war with him just because he seemed determined to pick a fight. Because she couldn't do that. She deeply regretted her past lies and the part she'd played in increasing his suspicion of women, and surely the only way she could make amends was to demonstrate her support for him in a quiet and caring way.

So she was determinedly upbeat on the way to the airfield to Alej's jet, and grateful for the large bedroom on board, which meant she was able to sleep for most of the night flight to Buenos Aires in the vast king-size bed. But Alej didn't join her and every time her eyelids fluttered open it was to find her husband sitting working on his laptop, seemingly oblivious to the hours which were creeping away. As morning broke in a firework explosion of coral and golden sunrise, she saw that he'd fallen asleep in the chair.

Sliding out of bed, she padded over to kiss his forehead and he awoke with a start, his gaze briefly disorientated before he seemed to gather his wits about himself. And not just his wits. He was hard for her and seemingly ready and so was she and she gave silent thanks that the plane's crew had their own private quarters at the other end of the giant aircraft as he ripped off her little satin teddy. Pausing only to unzip himself and push his trousers down far enough to free himself, he impaled her completely before kissing away her startled gasp of pleasure as he bounced her up and down on his lap. Was *this* all she meant to him? she wondered, just before she succumbed to the pulsing tide of pleasure which beckoned.

She was showered and dressed by the time their plane touched down—the faint flush of her cheeks and bright eyes the only outward sign of their lovemaking, though inside, her heart was pounding like mad. A chauffeur-driven car was waiting to take them to Alej's *estancia* and Emily drank in the sight of the Argentinian countryside. Last time she had been here, it had been for a brief and flying visit—jolted by running into Alej again and marred by Joya's ill health. This time it was different. Her head might be all over the place but in many ways she had found a curious kind of contentment, because didn't she actually *enjoy* her husband's company, as well as being completely bamboozled by the things he did to her in bed?

She was lost in her own thoughts when Alej pointed out the soaring shape of a distinctive mountain.

'They say it resembles the shape of a reclining woman. There's the curve of her breast and the—'

'I don't need a lesson in anatomy,' she cut in quickly.

'Well, any time you change your mind about that, I'm prepared to help you, Emily,' he taunted softly.

Blushing, she cleared her throat, aware of the chauffeur's dark gaze in the driving mirror and wondering if he spoke any English. 'So what made you buy a place out here?' she said, with a deliberate change of subject, as the luxury four-wheel drive began to descend into a green valley.

There was a pause before he spoke. 'If you look down there you can see exactly why.'

Emily blinked and then her eyes widened. She could. Nestled in a glorious dip and surrounded by beautiful mountains, she watched horses grazing happily in the lush emerald pastures, and the silver ribbon of a winding river as it meandered along. As the car bumped its way up the track towards the simply built wood-and-stone building, Emily felt her heart wrench with a powerful kind of longing. Because before her she could see something which she'd never really had. Something which felt like home.

The breath caught in her throat. 'Oh, Alej,' she said. 'It's beautiful.'

It was even more beautiful inside. Not eye-wateringly sumptuous like the apartment in Paris, but it had an air of quiet comfort, which was equally luxurious. The solid-looking furniture was designed to be used, not looked at, and the views from the giant windows were to die for. There were big skies with gusting clouds and rich, fertile soil with bags of space to run around in. Stupidly, she suddenly imagined children here, making joyful shouts as they played or rode their little ponies...

'The staff live in a house a little way down the track,' he explained, his deep voice butting into her suddenly painful thoughts. 'They leave me everything I need and only come if I call them, which isn't often, because this is a place for solitude—not people.' He nodded towards the kitchen. 'I'll make some coffee. You might want to take a trip upstairs. I've left a wedding present for you in the bedroom.'

She stared at him in surprise before a mild

stab of panic hit her. 'I haven't bought you anything.'

But he had already turned away. 'It doesn't matter. Go and see if you like it.'

Emily's heart was pounding as she ran upstairs and quickly found the master bedroom, which commanded the best views of all. And lying on the bed were a number of garments, which made her stop in her tracks. An exquisite pair of jodhpurs, a cream shirt of finest silk and a pair of brown riding boots in leather as soft as melted butter. And all in exactly her size. She didn't see the note at first, written in Alej's distinctive writing, and as she did she felt her heart clench with something like hope.

Put these on.

Her fingers were trembling as she did just that, not daring to dream that his gesture might mean what she wanted it to mean. Because the other night in bed—in those quiet and intimate moments after the heady hunger of sex had been satisfied—hadn't she told him that, yes, she missed riding, but that living and working in London made the pastime difficult. Just as she'd told him how much she missed the sweeping majesty of his homeland—and how it had been there, for the first time in her life, that she'd felt truly free. Had her words reminded him of the connection they'd once shared? Despite his immense power and wealth, was it possible that he yearned to re-capture some of that connection—or at least discover if such a thing were feasible?

She pulled on the soft leather boots and ran back downstairs to where the pungent aroma of strong coffee was wafting from the kitchen. Alej turned to watch her final descent, his eyes narrowing with a look she'd never seen there before, and didn't some imperceptible flicker in their verdant depths send a brief shiver tracking down her spine? She sucked in a deep breath, desperate to know what had prompted such a thoughtful gesture but terrified of say-ing the wrong thing.

'Thank you,' she said simply, because she couldn't really go wrong with that, could she?

He nodded as his gaze skated over her. 'You look…amazing.' He nodded towards the steaming pot, his words uneven. 'Help yourself to some coffee while I go and change. I thought we could ride out together. I have two horses saddled up and ready in the stables. That's if you're not too tired after the trip?'

Emily shook her head, unable to stem her

rising feeling of anticipation. 'Not tired at all,' she said eagerly. 'I'm tired of being cooped up inside and it's a long time since I was in the saddle.'

She drank her coffee and waited for Alej. He reappeared soon enough in jodhpurs which clung to his narrow hips and a shirt as fine as hers, which outlined the shadowy musculature of his torso, and Emily had to fight the urge to touch him. He led her out to the stables, where she saw a gleaming black stallion and beautiful golden mare, all saddled up and waiting to go, and her heart leapt with excitement at the thought of riding again after so many years. And then the groom appeared from within the gloom of the stable and his face was one she seemed to recognise. It was like a flashback, she thought—as past and present became confusingly combined, because he reminded her of her stepfather's elderly groom, Tomas.

'It's Tomas's son, Gaspar,' explained Alej, as if he had read her mind. 'He and his wife work for me now.'

Gaspar smiled and greeted her in Spanish before going back into the stable and when he returned, he was leading an old bay horse who began to whinny with pleasure as it came trotting across the yard towards her. Emily felt the prick of tears in her eyes as she threw her arms around his dear, familiar neck.

'Joya!' she said, burying her face in his well-groomed mane, and for a moment she thought she might cry. 'Oh, Joya. You look so…so *well*.' She lifted her face to meet Alej's hard green gaze, her voice shaky with gratitude. 'How can I ever thank you, Alej?'

His smile was brief as he shook his head, the firming of his mouth non-committal. 'No thanks are needed. I take pleasure myself in witnessing Joya's recovery, although, as he is too old for you to ride, you must be content with this palomino. Now let me see if you can remember what to do before I join you,' he said as he helped her up onto the saddle.

At first, Emily felt nervous and then exhilarated as she mounted the beautiful golden horse, but the main feeling which dominated was one of safety. Safe beneath Alej's watchful gaze, with his hand firmly on the rein as she trotted around the paddock. And wasn't it amazing how quickly it all came back—with confidence flowing through her by the second as she went through her paces? It wasn't long before Alej jumped on his own horse and Emily felt momentarily winded as she watched him ride. Because here was poetry in motion, she thought hungrily. Here was his skill and his gift perfectly demonstrated in a master-class of strength and symmetry, as he put the stallion through his paces.

They rode for an hour and Emily would have gone further, but Alej shook his head.

'Don't be greedy,' he said, his eyes as green as the lines of grass which bounded the silver river. 'That's enough for one day.'

So she dismounted, hot and a little sweaty, and as she did so she thought about what else she was greedy for. Her senses had been stimulated by the ride and now she wanted to make love. She wanted it with an urgency which never failed to take her by surprise, but today it felt more intense than usual. And once the groom had taken the horses and they had returned to the house, Emily reached for the man who had been a part of her life since she was twelve years old.

For the next couple of weeks, it was as if she'd found the life she'd always been secretly looking for. A simple life and a good life. Up early and out on the horses before being quickly swallowed up by the sweeping land-scape as they breathed in the fresh, Argentinian air. They ate al fresco and dangled their feet into the clear waters of the river and lit fires and barbecued fish. And whenever the opportunity arose, they explored each other's bodies—and each time was so intense that it was sometimes difficult for Emily to bite back the words of love she was longing to whisper in his ear.

Give it time, she urged herself, as he slid his rocky thigh between hers. Don't rush it. Let things settle, and heal, and who's to say what could grow between us if we nurture it? Maybe Alej wanted the same as her, though it was impossible to know what he was thinking or feeling and she didn't dare ask him and risk shattering the magic which seemed to have sprung up between them.

Afterwards, she found herself wondering how long that false state of affairs might have continued. How long it would have taken her to discover the horrible truth, if Tomas and Rosa hadn't decided to visit their only son, Gaspar. At the end of their two-day stay, Emily insisted on cooking them lunch, followed by *yerba maté* and sweet *alfajores* biscuits served on the veranda and, shortly before they left, she took Tomas down to the stables to see Joya.

'He is happy here,' the elderly groom pronounced, a huge grin splitting his creased face as the ancient bay came up to nuzzle him.

'Very happy,' Emily agreed.

'As are you.'

She wasn't going to deny it, not even to herself. And maybe the smile on her face told its own story. 'Yes,' she said quietly. 'I am.'

'Just as I am to see Señor Sabato settled and married at last,' said Tomas quietly, before giving a rueful shrug. 'And to think that if he hadn't decided to come to your stepfather's house that day, it might never have happened.'

Emily was in such a dreamy state that it took a moment or two for Tomas's words to sink in and when they did, she couldn't work out what he was talking about. 'But you were the one who emailed Alej,' she said.

'No, no,' Tomas negated, with a shake of his head. 'Señor Sabato contacted *me* first, to find out what time you would be visiting Joya.'

It didn't seem to make any sense at all and yet it made perfect sense. Or should that be *imperfect* sense? Emily wondered bitterly as an icy shiver ran down her spine.

It took every bit of concentration she had to say her farewells to Tomas and Rosa and to wait until she and Alej had returned to the house, before she dared confront him. And wasn't there a part of her which didn't *want* to confront him? Which wanted to carry on exactly as they were, no matter how false a situation it might be? She waited until he had pulled a beer from the fridge—declining the one he offered her.

'Tomas told me something strange today, just before he left,' she began slowly.

He flicked the top off the bottle, taking a long swallow before fixing her with his hard, green gaze. 'Oh?'

She licked her lips. 'He told me that he didn't contact you to ask for help with Joya. That you were the one who got in touch first.'

He raised his dark brows. 'And?'

'Why did you do that, Alej?' Her brow furrowed. 'Why were you the one who instigated the meeting?'

'Because I wanted to see you again.'

Still she clutched at straws—but then, wasn't it natural to grab at anything you could, when it felt as if you were drowning? 'To hire me, you mean? To use my PR skills to salvage your reputation and enhance your political ambition?' she added, just in case she hadn't made herself clear.

There was a pause. A long pause which suddenly felt like a shotgun being loaded.

'But I don't have any political ambition,' he said slowly.

Emily gazed at him with a feeling of desperation, as if they were both looking at the same picture on the wall but each seeing something different. As if she could see a boat and he could see a tree. 'Of course you do,' she said briskly.

'I don't,' he said simply.

'But you said—'

'I told you that to get what I wanted.'

'To get what you wanted,' she repeated, like someone learning a new language. She shook her head. 'You've lost me, I'm afraid. I haven't got a clue what you're talking about, Alej.'

'Then maybe I should tell you.'

'Maybe you should.'

Alej drank another mouthful of beer, leaning back against one of the worktops, his gaze fixed on the sudden stillness of her pale face. A shaft of guilt pierced at him, but he forced himself to disregard it. Why should he feel guilty? She'd treated him like a stud. Hell, she was *still* treating him like a stud. Even if the last few weeks had been good, the only reason she was here was because he'd offered her money and because he turned her on.

So tell her. Tell her just how gullible she's been.

'It started back in March, when I heard you

were in town for the reading of your stepfather's will,' he began softly. 'And I can't deny I was curious.'

Not just curious. The very mention of her name had stirred up all kinds of stuff inside him—stuff he'd thought he'd forgotten. Stuff he'd wanted to forget. Anger and resentment and bitterness, too. But most of all—when he had clicked onto the photo on the internet and seen her smiling face and golden hair—he had felt lust. That same powerful lust which had always overwhelmed him whenever he saw her. He remembered the kick to his heart and the way his mouth had dried as he'd stared at the sapphire glitter of her eyes.

'Okay,' she said cautiously, but her voice was still filled with confusion. 'You were curious. That figures.'

He shrugged, his fine silk shirt whispering against his torso. 'I saw your photo and I was intrigued. I decided I wanted to see you again. I'm sure you can imagine why.' He paused as he flicked her a look. 'So I had to work out a way of doing that.'

'Please tell me I'm not hearing this, Alej,' she said quietly.

'Oh, but you are,' he said, steeling his heart to the sudden tremble of her lips. 'I read that you were part-owner of a modest PR agency and figured you would probably find it difficult to turn down an obscenely well-paid project if it was offered to you on a plate. And so I decided to employ you, but first I had to work out a good reason for doing so. I was known for my playboy lifestyle and avoidance of commitment—but neither of those things had ever impacted negatively on my career before. So I decided I needed a new career, one where image *did* matter—and that's when Alejandro Sabato, the would-be politician, was born.'

Her lips opened into an expression of disbelief. 'You mean…you mean you never intended to run for office?'

He put the half-empty beer bottle down on the counter. 'Never. Politicians have never been my favourite people. Oh, I've been approached often enough in the past to get involved, but I've always preferred to channel my energies and money directly into my charitable foundations. The politician is just the middleman who takes his cut along the way.'

She walked over to the window and stared out in silence. 'And the marriage?' she questioned eventually, her back still to him. 'What was the point of that?'

'It guaranteed that you would stay for as

long as I wanted you,' he said. 'In fact, I quite enjoyed watching your enthusiasm as you planned it all, reinforcing my opinion that all women are suckers for a wedding. And on a practical level, a marriage of convenience meant I could rid myself of the tiresome play-boy handle, once and for all.'

She turned around then and her cheeks were even paler than before, making her eyes look like two huge sapphires which dominated her face. 'So you were lying to me all the time?'

He didn't flinch at her accusation. Why should he? Yet the clench of his heart was un-comfortable—as uncomfortable as acknowl-edging the pain which was glittering from her big blue eyes. 'Yes, I was lying,' he grated. 'Now you know how it feels.'

Emily didn't move from the window as a flood of conflicting emotions rushed through her, making her feel faint and light-headed. There was hurt, of course there was. Bitter hurt. And she felt foolish, too—for having walked straight into his cruel trap to get her into his bed and wreak some sort of revenge on her.

But she'd gone willingly, hadn't she? There had been no coercion on his part, and that chemistry of old had exploded as if they'd never been apart. Only this time, their relationship had been on a deeper level than before. Or so she'd thought. It hadn't just been about first love and sexual awakening. He'd confided to her about his mother. He'd laid his soul bare for her to see all the darkness there. And yes, he had lied—but he was right: she had done exactly the same. Did it matter? she wondered suddenly. Could their lies have simply cancelled each other out so that they could forget all about them and start over?

And then she shook her head as if to clear it, wondering if she was in danger of going completely mad. Because of *course* it mattered. She'd told him lies because she'd been young and scared and had been backed into a corner. She hadn't cold-bloodedly worked out some torturous form of revenge, as Alej had done. He'd plotted to get her back into his bed but he'd played with her emotions, too. All these days here when she had been lulling herself into a sweet and romantic dream about a tentative future—while Alej must have been quietly laughing at how stupid she was.

Had he let his defences down in order to manipulate her—to try to get her to fall in love with him all over again?

And hadn't he succeeded?

'You bastard,' she hissed, and suddenly it felt

as if something had broken inside her. As if her determination to do the right thing and say the right thing had all crumbled away. What a *dupe* she had been, she thought disgustedly. Hadn't she learnt the hard way that you could never rely on a man for your happiness? That her independent life and career was the only reliable path to contentment? There might not have been anyone since Alej—but neither had there been this tearing pain which made her heart feel as if it were splintering into a thousand tiny pieces. 'I may have been guilty of telling lies, but not of cold-blooded emotional manipulation,' she raged. 'And at least I had youth on my side. What was your excuse? Because you know what? I actually feel sorry for you, Alej.'

'Sorry for me?' he questioned furiously. 'This from the woman who married me purely for money?'

'What other reason would I have for wanting to marry you when you're so closed up and cold and don't dare to ever trust anyone?' she retorted. 'You're just stuck in some empty loop where all you can see is the negative. You can't seem to shake off the past and appreciate what you have right now. Well, thank goodness I saw this side to you before I—'

'Before you what, Emily?'

She shook her head, aware that she had almost given herself away, because she sure as hell wasn't going to feed his already massive ego by telling him she loved him. Because surely now her main goal must be to eradicate him from her mind, and from her life. 'None of your damned business! You know what I suggest you do? That you go and find your blood brother. You find him and meet with him—because that's something which might help you make sense of your past, since nothing else has worked. Oh, and you can keep *these*!'

She twisted the yellow-diamond engagement ring and the matching studded wedding band from her finger and threw them on the table, where they landed with a clatter. 'And in the meantime, I'd like a car to take me to the airport where I intend getting the first scheduled flight back to England. And don't even think about putting me on your private jet, Alej—because there's no way I'm setting foot on it.'

CHAPTER ELEVEN

IT WAS THE dullest day Emily could remember, but then she'd been particularly sensitive to adverse weather conditions of late. When you spent a lot of your leisure time staring out of the window, you tended to notice things like spattering raindrops and fog so thick that it looked as if the world were permanently shrouded in a grey blanket. Maybe she should be grateful that the world wasn't all bright and sunny. Imagine if the sun were shining and the sky bright blue—wouldn't that only emphasise just how dark her world was and how broken her heart?

She just missed him. So much. She hadn't factored that in when she'd stormed from the Argentinian billionaire's *estancia*, barely even gritting out a goodbye when the car had arrived to take her to the airport. And in the intervening weeks there had been nothing. No email, no phone call—not even a letter from his lawyer, announcing that he wanted a divorce. He probably wasn't even going to bother asking for a divorce, she thought gloomily. He could get one automatically in a couple of years on grounds of desertion and, in the meantime, his marital status might stop other women from trying to rush him to the altar. Being an estranged husband would only add to his inestimable appeal.

She kept repeating to herself that she would get over it sometime soon. And that surely his lies and manipulation were reasons enough to make her despise him? But somehow it didn't seem to work like that. Instead, she found herself remembering the way he had kissed her and the things he had told her. Things he'd never confided to another soul. Didn't that mean anything? No, it didn't, she reminded herself sternly. It meant nothing at all. It was game-playing Alej at his best—the politician who never was! The man who'd done his best to whittle away at her defences and manipulate her emotions.

Only her finances were giving her reasons to be cheerful—and on many different levels. She wondered if Alej had expected her to refuse the massive fee he'd paid to marry her—in which case, he was going to be disappointed! Ignoring Great-Aunt Jane's protests, Emily was using most of the money to help secure her elderly relative's new home in sheltered housing accommodation—and the peace of mind this gave them both was incalculable.

And business was suddenly doing very well indeed. She and Marybeth had acquired a steady stream of new clients, which had meant they'd had to take on an extra member of staff—a hard-working young woman called Sophie, who fitted in immediately. It wouldn't have taken a genius to work out that their new, super-cool reputation had come about as a result of mixing with a certain billionaire Argentinian. This naturally attracted lots of interest, yet somehow Emily's polite but detached attitude managed to stop the most avid questioners in their tracks. So that when someone inevitably enquired where her husband was, she would reply, 'He's away on business at the moment,' while daring anyone to ask more.

And nobody did. At least, not until Emily walked into the office one morning and Marybeth looked up at her with narrowed eyes.

'You haven't worn your wedding ring since you got back.'

'That's right.'

'Want to talk about it?'

'Nope.'

She didn't want to be one of those women who rehashed the whole heartbreak of a broken relationship to her friend, thus forcing herself to relive it, over and over again. And she didn't want Marybeth calling Alej names, because she was the only one who was allowed to do that. She had given it her best shot—that she had failed was down to the people they both were and the things which had happened to them. Her lies about wanting to sleep with other men had made him seek a primitive kind of revenge. Between them, they'd both helped destroy any possibility of a happy future together—even if Alej had shown any genuine signs of wanting one. Which he hadn't, Emily reminded herself painfully. He had let her go and was probably supremely happy about it. Even worse—she swallowed, trying to get rid of the rawness which had risen in her throat— he might even be back on the circuit, seducing and allowing himself to be seduced by the most beautiful women the world had to offer. Women he would never really trust, because his trust had been breached and his attitude warped by the lies he'd been told by his mother and by Colette. And by her.

But she knew she couldn't sit around pining for him for the rest of her life. She had to get out there and start living—even if her heart was hurting. She had to. She wasn't going to be like her mother, growing increasingly dependent on a bottle of tranquillisers to take the edge off a reality she didn't like. She had loved and lost, but it happened. It was all part of life.

'So what are you going to do now?' Marybeth was saying.

She looked at her friend rather sheepishly. 'I've started riding again. I realised how much I'd missed it.'

'You're joking?'

'Do I look like I'm joking? I can afford one lesson a week—I mean, it's not like I'm the biggest consumer in the world. There are actually riding stables in Hyde Park, which aren't as expensive as I thought.'

'Good for you.' Marybeth gave her a sly look. 'And I guess that means you'll get to wear those sexy new riding clothes you brought back from your honeymoon.'

The cold wind whipped around him and the rain was lashing so heavily that the short journey from limousine to apartment block meant Alej was as soaked as if he'd just been out sailing on rough seas. He scrolled down the list of names beside each corresponding doorbell until he came to the one which said Emily Green, and then jammed his thumb on the doorbell.

The silence which ensued was so drawn-out that he began to wonder if she was out, despite the assurances of a member of his London office, who had reported back that she'd finally arrived home from work. He glanced at his watch. He supposed she could be asleep already—but at *nine o'clock*?

And then he heard her voice through the intercom. Her soft and beautiful voice.

'Hello?'

'Emily. It's me.'

He supposed she didn't have to ask who, since everyone told him his accent was distinctive, but he wasn't anticipating the long silence which followed, before a strained voice asked a question so low that he had to dip his head forward in order to hear.

'What do you want?'

He wanted to feel her arms around him and his lips on hers, her soft body wrapping itself around him—that was what he wanted. But he wasn't really in an ideal bargaining position to state his demands, and certainly not from out here. 'It's raining and it's cold, Emily—'

'I don't need a meteorological report, thank you. If you don't like it then go back to Argentina—I believe the weather's more reliable there!'

'I'm not going anywhere until I've spoken to you.' He put his mouth close to the intercom. 'Now, we can do this one of two ways. You can let me in by pressing the buzzer or I can use a rather more unconventional means to grant entry, and if that involves kicking this door down then that's exactly what I'm going to do.'

'You wouldn't dare do that!' He could hear the bravado in her voice.

'You want to bet?'

The buzzer sounded and he pushed on the door quickly before it locked him out again, stepping inside to be bathed by the harsh light of the fluorescent strips overhead. Ignoring the elevator, he took the stairs two at a time until he arrived at her front door to find it slightly ajar. Cautiously, he pushed his way inside before shutting it quietly and heading towards the room from which light was streaming onto the wooden floor in the hallway. She was standing in a small sitting room, her back to him, staring out at the diamond glitter of the city lights in the night sky. She must have heard him enter but she spoke without turning round.

'Why are you here, Alej? What do you want?'

'I want to see your face so that I can talk to you.'

'Tough. You can talk to me this way.'

'Emily, please.' His voice dipped. 'What are you trying to hide?'

She turned around then and his pulse thrummed as he thought how different she seemed from the woman he'd said goodbye to just a few weeks earlier. Even in that short time her body seemed more honed and her cheekbones appeared sharpened as they cast shadows over her pale skin. And she'd had her hair cut. Not short, he registered, with grim relief, but the few inches which had been lopped off the flowing golden locks and the new, blunt-cut style made her look slightly aloof and very contemporary.

'I'm not trying to hide anything, but I see no need for further communication with you, Alej,' she said stiffly. 'So say what it is you came to say and then leave me in peace to get on with the rest of my life.'

Those last few words made him realise how much he had hurt her—more than he'd ever imagined. And, even more importantly, that he had no desire ever to do so again. But would she believe him if he told her that? Did he have any right to *expect* her to believe him after the things he had done? He walked across the room towards her. 'Please don't back away,' he said.

'I don't want you near me.'

'Okay.' That hurt, but he took it because he suspected he deserved it, sucking a breath which felt hot and ragged. And suddenly all the words he'd been composing in his head on the flight over seemed to form themselves into just three. 'I'm sorry, Emily.'

Her eyes looked very dark and very bright. 'Sorry for what? That you got found out? That Tomas rumbled you and let me in on your little secret sooner than you intended? Which makes me wonder just how long you were going to keep up the pretence of wanting to go into politics, Alej. Long enough for the thrill of having sex with me to wear off, I suppose?'

'In theory, yes—'

'You absolute b—'

'But in practice that day was never going to come around because I could never tire of you, Emily.' His fervent words cut through her fury. 'How could I, when I love you?'

She shook her head so that her hair swung

in a pale and silky arc around her shoulders. 'Don't you *dare* come out with things you don't mean!' she said fiercely.

'You really think I would lie about something like that?' he questioned. 'When I've always loved you—even though I've spent a long time trying to deny it to myself. It's why your lies hurt me more than any of the others. Fabrications came to my mother as easily as breathing, which wasn't really surprising, given her history. And Colette's lies meant nothing, not really. My relationship with her was never intended to be anything other than a no-strings affair. She was the one who wanted more. Who was prepared to write that vicious book about me when I wouldn't—or couldn't—give her what she wanted.' He took another step towards her and this time she didn't stop him. 'Can we start over?' he said simply. 'Will you be my wife in every sense of the word, Emily? Will you let me love you and cherish you, for as long as we both shall live?'

Emily looked into his bright green eyes and felt a quiver of hope begin to shimmer over her skin, but still she was wary because she was scared. Scared of what would happen if she let herself believe that what he said was real.

Scared of hurt and scared of pain. 'What made you come here today?'

Briefly, he closed his eyes and sighed as he opened them again. 'You forgot your necklace.'

She blinked. 'My necklace?'

He dug into his pocket and withdrew a battered box Emily instantly recognised, just as she did the fine gold chain and tiny pearl which lay inside—the necklace which had belonged to her mother.

'I rang up the office to speak to you and Marybeth told me you were helping your great-aunt move,' he continued. 'I remember you telling me that she didn't have a lot of money and so I put two and two together and guessed you'd used the payment I made when you married me.'

'And you were surprised I hadn't used it for my own greedy gain?' she said sarcastically.

'Hardly.' His lips curved into a sardonic smile. 'The contemptuous way you slung your wedding and engagement rings across the table was pretty indicative that you aren't one of the world's gold-diggers, no matter how much I initially wanted you to be. But the real reason I rang was that you'd changed your phone number and I wanted to talk to you and tell you how much I missed you. Wrong tense,' he corrected acidly. 'Miss you. Every second, every hour and every day. And I want to know whether we can try again. Whether you can forgive me for what I did and give us another chance.'

Emily saw the conviction which was blazing from his green eyes and could feel her heart racing as she hovered on the knife-edge of uncertainty. She knew what would be the safest option. To send him on his way, because love inevitably brought with it the potential for pain and if she stayed single she would be spared that. Oh, she might get bored or lonely—but she wouldn't be leaving herself open to the possibility of feeling as if someone had ripped her heart right out of her chest with jagged fingernails.

But that was a decision she was never going to make. It was a no-brainer, really. She loved him. Totally. She always had and always would. 'Of course I can,' she whispered shakily.

His quizzical green gaze met hers. 'Why?'

It was a seminal moment and Emily realised that she held the balance of power as she looked into his beloved face, which for once held a trace of insecurity, but the thought was lost the moment she went into his waiting arms because weren't they equals?

'Because I love you too, Alej. My darling, darling Alej,' she whispered. 'You are my man—you always were and you always will be. The only man for me.' She hesitated. 'And you aren't the only one to have made mistakes. I was wrong to let my mother and my stepfather pressure me into giving you up and it's something I've regretted ever since because—'

But he silenced her with his kiss and as the kiss deepened, the hurt and the pain began to dissolve. She was shaking with emotion and desire as he drew his head away, his hand skating slowly down the side of her face. 'Do you think you might like to show me where you sleep?' he questioned unsteadily.

'I think I might,' she answered, almost shyly.

It was much later, when they were lying in her rather cramped bed, wrapped in each other's arms, that she traced her finger over the outline of his lips. 'What about your brother, Alej? Did you find him? Did you even try?'

'Yes, I tried,' he said, turning his face towards hers. 'I've had a team of investigators working on it and every avenue they've explored, they've come up with a blank. But we will find him, Emily. Of that I am certain.' His voice grew husky. 'But now, can we talk of other things? Because I have something I need to do.'

Emily blinked as he got out of bed and fished around in the pocket of his jacket and pulled out another leather box—this one much less battered than the one which had belonged to her mother. And then he was getting down on one knee and prising open the lid and there, sitting on a bed of dark velvet, reposed a huge sapphire, surrounded by a glittering oval of diamonds. It was as if he had captured the dark ocean and poured it into the sparkling gem which almost blinded her.

'What's this?' she breathed.

'Your engagement ring.'

'But I've already got one. The yellow diamond?'

'Which I told you to choose from the internet,' he agreed darkly, as he slid the ring onto her trembling finger. 'Bad karma. So I picked this ring myself—mainly because the sapphire matches your beautiful eyes and because the diamonds are as bright as your spirit.'

It sat snugly on her finger but Emily paid it little heed for her attention was drawn by the far more beautiful image of the man who was kneeling before her. 'Oh, Alej,' she breathed, tugging at his shoulders to drag him back into bed, so that she could put her arms tightly around his neck and hug him. 'I love it, but not nearly as much as I love you—and if you don't kiss me very quickly I think I'm going to explode!'

EPILOGUE

'AND I AM very proud to declare this riding centre open,' Emily said. Her Spanish was now almost fluent again—but she guessed that was the beauty of having undergone an intensive course to brush up on the beautiful language she'd once excelled at.

There was a thunder of applause as the great and the good of Argentina greeted her declaration with prolonged applause and the children in the front few rows wriggled impatiently, eager to get out and start riding some of the fine horses which were waiting for them in the stables. Emily smiled as she sat down in her chair in the front row and waited for her husband to speak.

Today was the official opening of the riding school for disadvantaged children which she and Alej had established—right next to his brand-new polo school, which was situated just outside Buenos Aires. It was probably the single most rewarding thing Emily had ever been involved with and when she'd mentioned this to Alej, he'd told her he felt exactly the same. In fact, he was planning to involve himself with both schemes on a fairly regular basis, allowing his business empire to be run by the top people he had on his payroll, until the day came when he had a son or daughter of his own to take over when the time came, if they wanted to.

'You were great today,' Alej murmured once the celebrations were finally concluded and they were settled in the car which was taking them home.

Emily looked across at him, and smiled, thinking how stunning he looked in that charcoal-grey suit, with the top two buttons of his shirt undone to reveal a glimpse of olive skin.

'So were you,' she breathed.

'*Querida*, do you think we'll ever get bored with this mutual lovefest?' he drawled.

A glow of satisfaction rippled through her as she shook her head. 'Not in this lifetime.'

They were heading for Alej's *estancia*, to that simple stone-and-wood building by green pastures and a silver river, which had felt like home from the first time she'd seen it and still did. They had settled in Argentina as soon as they could, after the night Alej had turned up in London—wet from the rain and his face filled with something like vulnerability—before declaring his love for her. Emily had sold her small apartment and given the proceeds to the new riding school, so that it was as much her venture as Alej's. She'd also sold her share in the business to Sophie, who was proving a super-efficient replacement.

'A little too efficient,' Emily had confided ruefully to Marybeth, just before she'd left for her new life. 'You won't miss me at all.'

'Oh, I'll miss you, all right,' Marybeth had said, her voice sounding suddenly choked. 'But I'm coming out to stay with you after Christmas, don't forget.'

'As if. I'm laying on some Argentinian hunks specially for you!'

With Alej's arm around her shoulders, the journey to the *estancia* was smooth and surprisingly fast and once they had dismissed the chauffeur, it was just the two of them—with a free evening ahead. And once she'd been outside to check on Joya, Emily returned happily to the house.

'What shall we do now?' she questioned.

'Guess,' said Alej softly as he began to un-button her dress.

She nuzzled at his neck and nipped the lobe of his ear like a tiny animal and he laughed and carried her upstairs, despite her protests. 'You won't always be able to carry me, you know!' she exclaimed as he proceeded to lay her down on the bed.

'Yes, I will,' he vowed as he continued to undress her.

Emily didn't bother correcting him. At least, not then, when she was so involved in helping him out of his own clothes, and her heart was thundering by the time she felt his naked skin against hers. But as he stroked her body with his usual rapt and detailed fascination, his fingers halted in their slow circumference of her breast, and he frowned.

'Something is different about you, *querida*.'

Did he know her so well? She guessed he did. But she simply smiled and said nothing.

His brow creased with concentration as his fingertip circled the other breast. 'Are you?' he persisted, and the expression on his face when she nodded was one she would carry in her heart for the rest of her days.

'*Sí,*' she whispered. 'I'm having your baby, Alej.'

She could see his throat constrict. 'How far gone are you?'

'Just six weeks. But we were so busy with the move that I didn't notice at first.'

His gaze was much brighter than usual as he brought his mouth down to brush over hers, his deep sigh of contentment warm against her. '*Te amo,*' he said, somehow both fierce and gentle, all at the same time. '*Te amo*, Emily.'

And when he entered her, with breathtaking eroticism and infinite tenderness, Emily cried out with love and with joy and, very soon, with fulfilment.

For a long time afterwards she lay there trembling in his arms, her head pillowed on the rapid rise and fall of his chest, while he stroked her hair.

'It happened sooner than I thought,' she said reflectively.

He gave a low laugh. 'Judging by the amount of times we've been having sex, I'm surprised it hasn't happened sooner.'

'But we might not have been able to have children at all,' she ventured.

'Then we would have adopted. Or fostered.'

'Yes.' Her voice was still thoughtful. 'But I still think we've been very lucky.'

His fingers tangled in the silken tumble of

her hair, Alej looked up at the ceiling. Yes, she was right. Very lucky—that he had followed his instincts and sought her out, and that both their hearts had been big enough to forgive and to try again.

With his wife's gentle persuasion he had managed to forgive his mother for what she had done, and to let all the bad memories go. Because one day he wanted to tell his children about a woman who had sometimes sung when she was planting vegetables and who made the best *yerba maté* of anyone he knew. Because nobody was all bad, he'd realised—just as nobody was all good. The only faint shadow in his life was his lack of success in locating his sibling, but at least now he had discovered a name.

Lucas.

Lucas.

His heart clenched. Strange to think he had a brother. That someone, somewhere in the world shared his gene pool.

'Shall I get us something to drink?' asked Emily, her soft voice breaking into his thoughts.

He shook his head. 'You will do no such thing. From now on I will be waiting on you hand and foot, *bella*.'

'I'm not an invalid, Alej,' she scolded softly.

'No, you are my wife and the mother of my child.' He turned her face towards him. 'My beautiful Emily, who has taught me the meaning of love.'

'As you have me,' she said shakily. 'Just as you've taught me so much else besides. About acceptance and forgiveness. About strength in the face of adversity. And I love you too, Alej. I love you so very much.'

His arms tightened around her and the pounding of his heart threatened to deafen him. And as the setting sun turned the river into a ribbon of bright coral, Alej tilted Emily's chin so he could kiss her again.

* * * * *

If you enjoyed
Bought Bride for the Argentinian
by Sharon Kendrick
look out for the second instalment in the
Legendary Argentinian Billionaires duet
The Argentinian's Baby of Scandal,
coming soon!

And why not explore these other
Conveniently Wed! stories?

Crown Prince's Bought Bride
by Maya Blake

Chosen as the Sheikh's Royal Bride
by Jennie Lucas

Penniless Virgin to Sicilian's Bride
by Melanie Milburne

Untamed Billionaire's Innocent Bride
by Caitlin Crews

Available now!